. . ."Well, let's see what toys we have here on your list."

Kyle opened the note and began to read the "Dear Santa" aloud, but stopped as soon as he began.

Dear Santa,
Plez send me a daddy for Christmas so
Mommy doesn 't have to work so much.
Luv, Krissy Alexander

Kyle felt his chest tighten. This letter decided it. He was much too much of a sap for this job.

"You don't have a daddy, Kristen?" he asked softly as he re-folded the note.

"Nope. . ."

Martha —
I hope you enjoy this
little bit of New England.
Happy Holiday!
Lisa Mondello

All I Want for Christmas...is You!

by Lisa Mondello

Neighborhood Press

All I Want for Christmas...is You is a product of Neighborhood Press Publishing Company, Middleburg, FL.

ISBN 1-893108-01-5

Thank you to Maria Bernard, Tracy Ritts, Natalie Damschroeder, Jodi Israel and Beth Marshall for all your support and honesty.

A special thanks to my family for their belief and encouragement.

This book is dedicated to my husband Tom. Thank you with all my heart for your unwavering faith and love each and every day.

Love, Lisa

~1~

"Come on, Mommy!" Kristen Alexander said, tugging at her mother's sleeve. "There's no one in line this time."

"Wait a minute, honey. Let me tie your shoelace." Lauren Alexander squatted down and blew out a quick breath as she made a bow in the multicolor laces of her six year old daughter's sneakers. Kristen was as hard as ever to keep up with these days.

The shopping mall had been crowded all evening, filled with holiday shoppers carefully selecting their Christmas gifts. Scanning the area, she now saw only a handful of scattered shoppers left, carefully gripping their bundles. With less than three weeks left until Christmas, Lauren had hoped to be farther along with her shopping. This latest trip to the toy stores, meant as a fishing expedition to find out just what would catch Kristen's eye, had produced nothing but unrest. She'd hoped to make this a special year for Kristen. So far, it wasn't turning out to be what she'd planned. There was no way she would be able to afford the kind of Christmas she'd hoped to have.

"Mommy!" Kristen squealed, "I don't want to miss Santa Claus!"

"Okay, give me a kiss," Lauren requested, reaching out to

give her a brief hug. Smiling, Kristen quickly obliged. "Do you want me to go with you, baby?"

"No-o-o-o!" Kristen said, rolling her eyes at her mother.

"I know you're a big girl now, but I had to ask. I'll be standing right at the end of the ramp, okay?" Lauren assured her, feeling a tug at her heart. Her little girl was so grown up at six years old. Time was flying by so fast. She only wished she had more time to spend with Kristen to watch her grow.

Kristen trotted up the ramp a few feet and stopped short, abruptly turning and racing back. "My letter for Santa! Mrs. Hopkins helped me with it. I forgot it at home!" she cried with all the panic of a little girl who'd just lost her kitten.

"No, Krissy, I have it. Mrs. Hopkins gave it to me when I picked you up after work. Remember?" Lauren pulled the sealed envelope marked "North Pole" out of her purse and handed it to Kristen. "Go on. The mall is going to be closing soon."

Kristen's exasperated expression was replaced with a chubby faced smile as she clutched the letter to Santa in her little hand and bolted up the ramp.

Thank the heavens above for Mrs. Hopkins, Lauren thought. If she didn't watch Kristen before and after school every day, she couldn't have taken that job at Woodlawn Industries as a customer service representative. She'd still be waiting tables and paying baby-sitters top money just to make ends meet. At least now, she had a chance to make something for herself and Kristen. The Woodlawn position offered her the chance for advancement and training she never would have gotten if she'd remained at the restaurant she'd worked at since leaving home.

She watched Kristen race to meet Santa, determined to tell her Christmas wish. She sighed, feeling her heart fall. If only she had the money to give her all the things she wanted.

Kyle Preston watched as a little blue eyed cherub of a girl, no more than a first grader, came racing up the ramp toward him. It was as hot as a burning August day in this Santa Claus suit. He'd been wearing it for the last three hours and was soaked skin deep from his boots to his white beard. He needed a shower and a good meal. To say that he was tired was the understatement of the century, but seeing the delightful sparkle of a child at Christmas was worth all the hassle and discomfort of playing Santa Claus.

"Ho! Ho! Ho!" he called out as the little girl came bustling toward him. Extending his hands in front of him, he gently lifted her into his lap. "And what's your name, little one?" he asked in his disguised Santa Claus voice.

The little girl looked up at him with wide saucer eyes and murmured softly, "Kristen. But my mommy calls me Krissy."

"That's such a pretty name for a pretty little girl. Have you been a good girl for your mommy this year, Kristen?"

"Yep. Sometimes I don't pick up my toys before bed though. Am I gonna get in trouble with you for that?" She didn't look at him. Instead, she stared off down the ramp where a woman in a bulky blue coat stood waiting. Seeing no one else in the vicinity, Kyle presumed it to be her mother.

"Is it all the time, or do you just forget once in a while?" he asked with Santa Claus authority.

"I thought you were 'spose to know those things? Mommy always says you can see me when I don't listen." She looked up at him wide eyed and innocent.

He chuckled, despite himself, in his normal tone. Then remembering his part, he altered his voice and ho-ho'd a laugh that made Kristen giggle. "Well, Kristen, it's too big a job to look at all the kids all over the world. So I have to ask for a little help every now and again. You don't mind that, do you?" He posed the question not expecting a reply, but to his surprise, Kristen looked up at him thoughtfully, contemplating her answer.

"I don't mind. Mommy needs help sometimes, too," she said as innocently as an angel.

He was too much of a sap for this job, he decided. Maybe it was his nature or maybe it was growing up in an ever expanding family, but he had a soft spot for this little girl. She was cute as a button with her baby fine blond curls framing her face. Looking down the ramp, he decided her mother wasn't half bad herself. She appeared a bit tired, but pretty in a simple girl-next-door kind of way. Her flowing ash blond hair fell both to the front and back of her knee length coat. Even from the distance they were at, he recognized that mother and daughter bore a strong resemblance and had the same saucer shaped eyes.

Kyle turned his attention back to the pressing matter at hand and asked, "So, what do you want for Christmas this year?"

Kristen's little face brightened even more, if that was at all possible, and she stuck out the envelope she'd been crumbling nervously in her hand. "Here. I wrote it down so you won't forget."

"Well, I'm impressed. You did this all by yourself?"

"Mrs. Hopkins helped me."

He took the envelope and, after breaking the seal, plucked out the note. "Is Mrs. Hopkins your teacher?"

"Nope." She shook her head back and forth with exaggerated motion. "She's my baby-sitter. We live on the top floor of her house. She plays Barbies with me when Mommy can't cuz she has to work."

"Well, let's see what toys we have here on your list." Kyle opened the note and began to read the "Dear Santa" aloud, but stopped as soon as he began.

Dear Santa,

Plez send me a daddy for Christmas so Mommy doesn't have to work so much.

Luv, Krissy Alexander

Kyle felt his chest tighten. This letter decided it. He was much too much of a sap for this job.

"You don't have a daddy, Kristen?" he asked softly as he re-folded the note.

"Nope."

"What happened to him?" he asked, immediately doubting the wisdom of putting forth such a question to someone so young.

"We never had one. Mommy says we do just fine as a twosome. That means just Mommy and me," she clarified, nodding her head with certainty.

"Oh. You're pretty smart for a girl your age."

"I know. Mommy tells me so all the time," she said unabashed.

"What's your mommy's name?"

"Lauren Alexander. She's over there. Hi, Mommy!" Kristen waved her hand frantically. The woman at the end of the ramp beamed with pride and waved back.

"Your mommy is very pretty," Kyle said mostly to himself when he saw how Lauren Alexander's beautiful wide smile brightened her face and made what he mistook as being simple much more appealing.

"Yep," she answered as if the point was not debatable.

He looked down at Kristen and smiled. "There must be some toy you'd like Santa...uh...me to bring you Christmas morning."

"Nope. Just a daddy. I think my mommy could use it."

Kyle couldn't help but laugh at the double meaning of her words. "Glad to see you're looking out for your mommy, Kristen. But what about you?"

"I never had a daddy." Her eyes narrowed in as she frowned. "So I don't know. Does that mean you're not gonna get us one?"

Kyle had spent the first twelve years of his life being shifted around until he found a family that would love him no matter what. The most impressionable years of his life were spent thinking no one cared, that he was nothing special. Looking at Kristen, he knew she was special, but did she?

And Lauren Alexander. Obviously she was alone, raising her daughter the best way she could. It had to be a hard thing to have no one to lean on.

Looking back on his life, Kyle realized he'd pretty much forgotten what that had been like. These days, as far as family went, his cup runneth over. There were a lot of people to do the leaning and even more to do the leaning on in the Preston household. Yeah, it had to be hard for Lauren Alexander if her young daughter felt it necessary to give her Christmas wish away.

"No, Kristen. That doesn't mean you're *not* going to get a

daddy. It's just..." he started, but couldn't quite find the words to explain the complications involved in such a request. Especially when Kristen looked up at him with wide puppy-dog eyes.

Why couldn't she have asked for an Easy Bake Oven?

All of the sudden, he found himself feeling abundantly protective of Kristen and her mother. This was, after all, the holiday season. It was a time when all should reach out to their fellow man, woman, or as in this case, child.

He tried a different tactic, hoping the little girl would quickly see the flaw in her request and ask for something more Santa Claus possible. "Don't you think that your mommy would want to pick out a daddy on her own? What if she doesn't like the daddy that I bring?"

Kristen looked puzzled. Exactly what he'd wanted, although he had to admit to himself that he didn't enjoy trading innocence for the turmoil in her expression. He just couldn't see any other way around this without flat out telling her he couldn't do it. That would be like telling her that Santa Claus didn't exist at all and there was no way he'd be the one to say such an evil thing.

"But Mommy doesn't have any time to find a daddy. That's why I figure it's up to me." She nodded her head with determination.

If there was any way to bottle that kind of pure love and devotion, he'd do it. That soft spot was turning to mush as Kyle felt his heart grow warmer with every thump. He knew he couldn't do his usual routine and tell the child that she'd only get her wish if she was real good and picked up her toys when asked. In the end, she'd only surmise that she'd done something wrong for Santa not to grant her Christmas request.

"I can tell you love your mommy a whole lot," he murmured softly.

Kristen nodded her reply. A weary smile tugged at her mouth. Or maybe she was tired, he thought, remembering the time. The mall was closing at any moment. The grilled gates had already been slammed down and locked up on the front of some stores. Custodians were busy emptying the trash cans and vacuuming the carpets. As Kyle panned the area, he saw that the last remaining shoppers had already vacated the premises.

Turning his attention back to Kristen, who was now yawning as she lazily leaned against his chest, he said, "I can't make any promises for this year, honey. Being so close to Christmas, all the daddy's have already been spoken for. But I'll see what I can do for next year," he promised.

He wasn't at all pleased with his answer. What he wouldn't do to make Kristen's dream come true? He looked down the ramp at Lauren Alexander. She gave him a forced smile that hinted of impatience as she shifted her weight from one foot to the other, her hands jammed in her coat pockets.

"You be the good girl I know you are and there will be something extra special for you on Christmas morning. Okay?"

It was late. He was hot as hell. He had to get home, have a hot shower, and grab a good meal.

But none of that mattered, because now he just felt like a dog. Why couldn't she have asked for a puppy? he thought as he watched her trot toward her mother. He could have easily run right down to the pet shop at the mall and picked out a golden retriever, or collie, or whatever kind of puppy looked cute as a button, just like Kristen. Instead, she asked for the one thing a Santa had no control over.

There were times in his life when Kyle had known failure. Going from nothing to being the owner of his own shopping mall in Western Massachusetts had given him cause to stare failure right between the eyes. But in all his thirty years, he never felt as low and pitiful as he did right now.

His appetite suddenly gone, he decided the heck with the dinner. He changed out of his straight jacket and called it a day.

Lauren turned the key in the ignition for the second time and said a silent prayer that the car's engine would turn over.

Nothing.

"Not now," she moaned, a sinking feeling flooding her. She'd already secured Kristen in the back seat and fastened her seat belt. A quick glance in the rear view mirror showed that the little girl had already fallen asleep.

She popped the lever that released the hood of her late model sedan and noticed the light panel. Her hands instinctively pushed the knob on and off in frustration when she realized she'd left her lights on the entire time she'd been shopping. Her battery was dead.

She lifted the hood and blankly stared down at her car engine feeling the bitter cold sting her exposed cheeks. Taking in another frosty breath, she realized she had no idea what she was looking at and no idea what to do. Cursing, she kicked the air in frustration.

To add insult to injury, it had begun to snow while she'd been in the mall. Any other time it would have brought out the playful spirit of Christmas in her. She'd always loved a white blanket of snow on the ground during the Christmas season. She glanced over at Kristen and saw that she was already fast asleep, slumped over in the back seat. The snow was going to make it more difficult to carry her to a pay phone and call a tow truck, but she had no other choice. The temperature had dropped considerably in the few hours they'd been shopping and it wasn't safe to stay exposed for too long.

Twisting her body around, she saw that the parking lot was empty. At least she'd parked in a well lit area just below a lamppost, something working late nights at the restaurant had taught her to do many years previous. As she gazed up at the bright light above her, she became hypnotized for a fleeting moment by the colors of the dense snow falling like crystals from the sky.

"You stuck?" a deep voice, one that sounded much too close for comfort, called out and startled Lauren, causing her to swing around.

She licked her chapped lips and stared at the tall man who had seemingly come out of nowhere. His hair was wet and matted, colored a mousy blond. He was hunched forward slightly with his hands shoved deep into the pockets of his sporty ski jacket.

"No," she lied. The last thing she needed was some deranged wanderer to come by and steal what little she didn't have. Lauren quickly shifted her thoughts to Kristen, sleeping in the back seat. He could take anything he wanted, but she'd walk through fire to protect her precious daughter from harm.

"Interesting," he returned, darting a glance in the direction of her exposed engine.

"What is?" She tried desperately to not appear frazzled.

"Well, I'm no expert, but I have never known someone to fill their engine with snow before taking it out for a drive," the stranger said teasingly, his hot breath misting as it hit the cold air. He moved to the front of the car, half out of her view, presumably looking at the engine.

Crow bar! That's what she needed now, she decided. If she only knew where it was kept in her car, she was sure she could make good use of it if need be. It was not time to beat herself up about not paying attention during Drivers Ed class. Something else to thank Kristen's father for at some later date since he was the subject of her attention during that fateful time in her life. In any case, it didn't stop her stomach from lurching forward with every move this stranger made.

The man stuck his head out from behind the hood. "Nothing seems to be disconnected. Let me try the engine."

"That won't be necessary," she blurted out. There was no way she was going to let some stranger climb into her car and drive away with her baby. In an attempt at bluffing, she informed him, "I've already called my husband and he'll be here any minute."

"No he won't." The aplomb in his voice, more than his words, told her that he was not convinced.

She struck a threatening pose with her arms held out in front of her, fists clenched, and shouted, "Don't come any closer. I'm a black belt in Karate."

He glanced at her blankly and darted his eyebrows upward. "No you're not."

Lauren's pulse quickened and she nervously shifted her body weight from one foot to the other, grounding herself in. The mama bear in her reared up and her claws stretched out in full fighting force. Just let him try to take her little cub away. She'd make sure it was the sorriest day of his pathetic life.

He shot her a mocking grin that tilted ever so slightly. "Why don't you use some of that heat to fire up the engine?"

"Huh?" Her heart pounding in her chest, Lauren unclenched her fists and stepped back toward the driver's side door.

"Try turning the ignition."

"What do you want?" she asked suspiciously, her guard never faltering.

"You don't have to be afraid. I just want to help you and your daughter get home before you freeze to death out here."

A bone chilling fear shot up her spin. He hadn't been close enough to see a child in the back seat. How could he have known? "Are you stalking me? I have a gun, you know. And I won't hesitate to use it!" She stuck her thumb and her index finger out and aimed it at the most sensitive part of his male anatomy, sneering at him.

"I believe you would," he said. Tilting his head to one side, he blew out an exaggerated breath, emitting a cloud of mist from his mouth. "But if you're going to bluff, at least try to be a little more convincing. Right now, you're about as threatening as a kitten."

"Kittens have claws," she warned, flexing her fingers.

"Cats have claws," he amended. "You, my sweet, are still a kitten."

Lauren straightened her spine and huffed. "I'm going to scream. Is that threatening enough for you? The security guards will be more than willing to arrest you on the spot and throw your sorry butt in jail for...for..."

"Helping you? No, they wouldn't do that," he said confidently.

"What makes you so all mighty sure, *buster*?" she shot back, verbally attacking him. Nothing else seemed to make a dent in him and she was running out of bluffs.

"Because I'm the one who signs their pay checks." He turned back at the mall and extended his hand. "I own this place."

"No you don't!" she challenged. She wasn't born yesterday. On her own since she was pregnant at eighteen, Lauren knew a snow job when she saw one.

He blew out another quick breath and shrugged. When he moved his hand toward his back pocket, Lauren screamed loud and long.

He stopped dead in his tracks. "What on earth did you do that for?"

"Don't try anything funny!" she commanded, holding her hands out in front of her as a shield.

Ignoring her, he extracted his wallet. After sifting through it, he plucked out what appeared to be a business card and extended it to her. "See for yourself. Kyle Preston, owner of Preston Galleria."

She quickly glanced at the card in his hand without taking it, then followed his gaze to the sign on the two story building behind him.

"How do I know you're legit?" she asked, still leery of accepting his story. She'd been a fool once when she was young, taking every little word as being the truth. That only left her alone, struggling to make a life for her and Kristen. She couldn't afford to keep making that mistake.

"I assure you that my intentions aren't mercenary. Please, just get behind the wheel and try to start the car. If my instincts are right, all you have is a dead battery," he said evenly, seemingly tired of the game.

"I know that's all it is." She folded her arms across her chest, feeling pretty proud of herself for at least figuring that one on her own. "I left my lights on."

"Oh. Good," he said in resignation. "Then I'll jump you."

"Not on your life!" She struck her Karate pose and ground her teeth, the mama bear in her coming to life again.

When he caught the double meaning of his words, he revised, "I'll bring my car around so that I can jump start your car's battery."

With that, he was gone. Lauren wasn't sure if he'd come

back after the way she'd attacked him. Kitten, my butt, she fumed. She had claws just like the next cat.

Kyle was gone for what seemed liked hours, but were only a few minutes. The cold may have had a hand at the slow passing of the time. She couldn't feel her toes in her boots anymore.

What would it hurt to accept some help from a stranger? she thought as she moved to the back of the car. She'd conditioned herself not to trust anyone in the past seven years. Maybe she was becoming too hard, too cold. And although Kyle Preston looked like he'd been put through the proverbial ringer when he appeared out of thin air, he did seem sincere about just wanting to help.

And it was more than that, she had to admit to herself. Except she couldn't quite put a finger on what it was about Kyle Preston that made her think she should trust him. Without something tangible for her to grasp on to, trusting was a dangerous thing to do to say the least.

After inserting the key in the lock, she opened the trunk and pulled out the blanket she kept there for just this type of emergency. She was just placing the blanket over Kristen when she saw headlights approach. The vehicle stopped head to head with her car and Kyle jumped out.

"Why don't you sit in your car. You'll be warmer. I'll only be a minute," Kyle said as he opened the hood of his Jeep and began connecting jumper cables.

Lauren slid into the driver's seat and rubbed her hands together, thankful that this ordeal would soon be over. She blew a hot breath through her frozen fingers before positioning them on the frigid steering wheel as she waited.

"Ready?" she called out the crack in her window after hearing a car door slam.

There was a sudden roar of the Jeep's engine. Then Kyle hollered, "Go ahead and try to start her."

Lauren turned the key in the ignition once. The Ford whined in protest until, finally, the engine turned over. She felt herself release the breath she hadn't realized she'd been holding. "Thank

God," she whispered, looking up at the ceiling of her car.

"You should run it for a few minutes before trying to drive. Let the battery get a little more juice." Kyle quickly removed the wires conjoining the two cars and closed the hoods.

She floored the gas pedal to warm the engine and turned on the heat in the car before getting out.

"I don't know how to thank you," Lauren said softly. Embarrassment flooded her with the memory of the way she'd behaved earlier.

"No need. You're all set now." Kyle smiled warmly. As he spoke, the sound of his resonant baritone voice soothingly settled her fear. She looked at him and, for the first time, she felt completely at ease. His face was kind, his smile was warm and she realized that he meant what he said, he only wanted to help.

"I apologize for the way..." she started, staring down at the inches of snow on the ground that had accumulated during the short time.

As if sensing her embarrassment, Kyle broke in and said, "Like I said. There is no need. Good will toward men and all that holiday cheer. Woman in your case, Ms. Alexander. You and Kristen are all set now." His eyes grew bright as he gazed at her. Despite the calming effect the deep timbre of his voice gave her just a few short moments ago, she now felt as if she'd just been struck by a bolt of lightning.

Fear racked her body causing her to shudder. "How do you know my name? M-my daughter's name?" she stammered, not missing a beat. She hadn't told him, but he knew. That feeling of ease was short-lived. She trembled, more fearful than she'd been earlier when she foolishly bluffed.

Kyle dug his hand deep into his denim clad pocket and extracted a crumpled piece of paper and held it out to her.

"What's this all about," she blurted out, her eyes fixed on his hands, her breathing becoming shallow.

"You don't have to be afraid. This will explain it all. I promise you." He smiled warmly and Lauren wanted to trust him if only to believe in simple kindness.

With shaking hands, she took the piece of paper, warm from being in the pocket close to Kyle's body. She held it up straight so that she could see Kyle while reading the words on the paper. "Dear Santa..." she read out loud, then read the next part silently. "Oh, no," she moaned.

"I know. That's just how I felt."

Lauren shot him a skeptical glance. "How did you get this?"

"Kristen gave it to me."

"That's impossible. Mrs. Hopkins just helped her with it this afternoon and-"

"And she gave it to me in the Mall," Kyle finished for her.

She looked at him quizzically, still trying to comprehend the course of events leading up to his seizure of her daughter's precious note.

"It's not that hard to figure out, Lauren," Kyle said warmly. His dark eyes gleamed with the light from the lamppost. He wore no hat to protect his head from the falling snow. Now his hair was filled with powdered flakes, matting it down. His grin was bright and wide as he informed her, "I'm Santa Claus."

~2~

In all her twenty-five years, Lauren thought she'd heard almost every line imaginable from a man. She was wrong. This one took the cake.

"And I'm the good witch of the North," she said sarcastically, trying to keep her voice steady. "Did you pick this up in the garbage or something?"

"I know you don't believe me-"

"You're right. I don't."

"I am telling you the truth."

The truth. Where had she heard that before? We love you no matter what, her father had told her. I'll always stand by you, Kristen's father had promised her. In the end, they both let her down by not keeping their word. The truth stung like a honey bee protecting its hive when it turned into a big, fat lie.

"Sure. Well, thanks for your help, anyway." She turned to move away, but his heavy sigh caused her to turn around again. She saw the defeated resignation in his expression and said, "You're telling me the truth, aren't you?"

"That's what I said." He smiled as he lifted his hands in the air and let them fall against his side.

She decided Kyle Preston had a nice smile, completely void of hidden intentions. She knew she had no reason to doubt his words. It had just been too many years of mistrusting and keeping her guard up so high that the old habit was hard to break.

"What did Kristen...my daughter say to you?" She wasn't quite sure what had prompted Kristen to ask for a daddy from Santa Claus. Lauren found her own insecurity forging her on to ask for more information.

"She said you work too hard." He spoke delicately, as if her hearing the words might break her, which it did. "She wanted you to have some help. And she said she loves you very much."

Lauren felt a smile tug at her lips. Her heart filled beyond capacity. She loved her little girl with all her heart and soul. She also felt Kristen's love back at her ten fold. It was so much like her to think of her mommy.

"I always thought I was doing a good job taking care of her, you know. But here she is trying to take care of me." Lauren looked down at her boots and bit her bottom lip, feeling the chapped skin peel. She nervously kicked a layer of powdered snow in frustration.

Not once had she ever heard Kristen mention wanting a daddy. She always thought of the two of them as a team, a twosome. Guilt crept through her veins with the realization of what Kristen obviously felt she was missing in her life, something Lauren alone couldn't give her. Even more so because she felt the need to ask someone else about it, instead of her own mother.

She asked Santa Claus no less!

Lauren felt a burning in the pit of her stomach. If Kristen couldn't tell her about wanting a daddy, then what else was she missing in her life that Lauren couldn't provide? A familiar anxiety swept through her, leaving her trembling. It was the same fear she felt when she boarded the bus to leave her hometown when Kristen was just days old. Back then, she wondered if she'd made the right decision for Kristen. And now, with Kristen feeling the way she did, she had to wonder if maybe she hadn't.

"Why don't we get some coffee or hot chocolate," Kyle suggested. "It's way too cold for us to be standing here discussing this."

"I have to get Kristen home. It's late and she has school tomorrow." Lauren blinked back a hot tear and sniffed. "Thank you for all your help, Kyle." She extended her hand intending to shake his in thanks.

He obliged by taking her hand in his. But to her surprise, instead of a simple hand shake, he tenderly squeezed it, holding on for a lingering moment. "If you ever need anything, don't hesitate to call me. Kristen's a great kid."

"Yes, she is." Lauren swallowed hard in an effort to clear the lump lodged in her throat. Too overwhelmed by Kyle's kindness to say anymore, she felt her bottom lip quiver.

"Take my card. Keep it handy. Please." He held out his hand and the business card with his phone number.

Lauren blinked hard and shook her head. "We're fine. Thank you very much for your help." She took a deep breath and opened the car door.

The warm car felt inviting when she finally plopped into the driver's seat. After fastening her seat belt, she turned around to find Kyle standing by her door peering into the crack of the open window.

"Tomorrow night there's a tree lighting ceremony in the town square. You may have heard about it on the local news," he said in one breath as if he thought she would flee before he had a chance to finish. The thought had crossed her mind.

"Yeah, I think I remember hearing something about it." Lauren revved the engine.

"There'll be a Santa for the kids. They're having a sleigh ride, hot chocolate, cookies and-"

"Why are you telling me this?" she asked.

He appeared taken aback by her question. She hadn't meant it to sound so blunt, but apparently it had. "Because I thought it would be a nice thing for Kristen...and for you. Things can get so hectic sometimes that we forget to stop and enjoy life, live a little."

This time, his words stung. "Is that what she said?" she asked. Her bottom lip quivered uncontrollably and a single tear betrayed her strength.

"Mrs. Hopkins plays Barbie dolls with her because you have to work." His face was serious, but not judgmental, she observed. He knew too much of the truth for Lauren not to believe that Kristen actually confided those secrets to him.

With the last bit of her resolve eaten away, Lauren burst into tears. Kyle opened the car door and, leaning in, he rubbed her back as she sobbed.

"I didn't mean to upset you...I just..."

Damn! Kyle cursed inwardly. He tenderly placed his arm around her shoulder in an attempt at comfort. What he wanted to do was pull her into his arms and hold her until she felt better, but given her earlier response, he thought better of it. Without actually walking in her shoes, he knew how she felt. He'd already been there on another level when he had no one to call his own.

In the warmth of the car, the scent of her drifted to him, invading his senses. It was fresh and clean like a clear day after a snow storm, yet there was something sultry that struck a cord deep within him. He cursed himself silently for the stirring it caused. Yeah, maybe it had been a while since he'd had a woman in his life, but he wasn't in the habit of seducing a defenseless creature like Lauren. He wasn't about to start now no matter how silky her hair looked. Or how fragrantly the scent of her filled his head. She tucked a lock of hair behind her ear exposing high cheekbones framing her eyes and that was the final straw. He pulled himself to a stand to regain his composure.

Lauren dropped her hands from her face and swiped away the tears with one quick motion. "I'm going to wake up Kristen if I don't stop this." She sniffed back a few more tears and reached over to shut the door. "Thank you again."

He caught the door with his hand. "What about the tree lighting ceremony? Will I see you there?" he asked, surprised at feeling a little more hopeful with the idea of seeing Lauren again.

"No."

"Come on. You can't just work for the rest of your life and-"

"I'm married," she blurted out, looking straight into his eyes.

"Oh." He blew out a mist of breath in confusion. His eyes inadvertently glanced at her left hand. "I'm sorry. I didn't see a ring and after what Kristen said..." He let his voice trail off trying to make sense of all the events that transpired over the evening and where he'd gone wrong. Why had Kristen told him she never had a daddy? And if that was true, then why was Lauren telling him she had a husband? It just didn't make sense.

The uncertainty in her eyes hit him like a hammer to a nail and it all made sense. "You're bluffing again, aren't you? You're not really married," he said softly.

She wilted right before his eyes, her shoulders sagging and she let out a slow breath. "No, I'm not. Kristen never knew her father," Lauren offered. She turned her face away and gazed out the windshield, seemingly mesmerized by the windshield wipers pushing the new fallen snow aside. "He's been out of the picture since before she was born. I guess that's why she wants a daddy. She never had one."

"I'm sorry," Kyle said in sympathy. The guy was a louse. But then again, he'd known just that type of louse when he was a kid. The only difference between Kristen and himself, was that Kristen had never known her father's rejections. Kyle had been old enough to stand in the courtroom and hear his own father denounce him as his son.

He pushed the horrid memory aside. Too many years had passed since that painful moment in his life. Too many good things had come into his life and taken its place. He hadn't always seen things that way, but thank God he'd wised up enough to finally see the light.

"Don't be sorry. I'm not. Kristen and I do just fine by ourselves," Lauren indicated, that same wildcat determination he'd seen earlier coming back to life in her expression.

Kyle figured it was true, but not by way of an easy road. What he wouldn't do to make things just a little bit easier for her.

"I see." Kyle felt a strange distance forced between them. The purr of both car engines seemed to grow with intensity as each second passed. "About tomorrow night, how about it?"

"No, I don't think so. I have to do...something." She tossed her hand in the air, giving it a fleeting second of thought, then added. "I have to wash my hair, do my taxes...something."

"Taxes?" he questioned under his breath, his eyebrows raised.

"Okay, I know it's not the greatest excuse," she admitted, fixing him with a stare, "but it's the best I can do. You seem like a nice person and you've been very kind, but I don't want to get involved with anyone. I'm just not interested in-"

"We're talking hot chocolate and a Twinkie. Maybe a few Christmas songs, if you can keep a tune. Even if you can't, we don't discriminate. We're not talking marriage." He couldn't keep the smile from creeping into his expression.

"Are you trying to tell me you weren't just coming on to me?" she asked, cocking her head to one side. The tears were gone now, a hint of a smile now adorned her face.

Kyle found himself with a mixed sense of protectiveness for her vulnerability and attraction because her lips suddenly looked so kissable. He hadn't intended the invitation to be a come on, but giving it a second thought, maybe it was. Put on another track, he decided he wouldn't mind it if she thought he'd made the pass. He'd like it even better if she'd accept.

"Yes," he lied. "I mean, I asked because I thought it might be a fun mother/daughter thing, a way for you to spend some fun time together during the holidays. Everyone has a good time."

She blinked and appeared uncertain, maybe even a little disheartened. "Good," she said, turning her gaze from his face.

"Would that be such a bad thing?" he asked, hoping to get some insight into that flicker of disappointment he saw flash across her face.

She pulled at the car door gently as a hint for him to move aside. "It's cold and I really do have to get Kristen home. Thank you again, Kyle."

"My pleasure."

He watched her drive away, the red tail lights of her late model car blurring into a cloud of falling snow. She's just another woman, he told himself. A beautiful woman with eyes like the full moon and full lips made for stealing a sweet kiss. It had been a long time since he'd thought along those lines. Pulling his fingers through his ice laden hair, he decided it had been way too long.

Kyle walked through the crowd of chatting locals gathered for the annual tree lighting ceremony, no doubt gossiping about their own neighbors or whoever was up for selectman at the next election. Bringing the town together brought out the good and bad in everyone. Kyle liked to think that it was mostly the best. He groaned inwardly remembering the mischief that came out of him in his youth when everyone was congregated here for the Christmas festivities.

Well, that was then, he mused. It had been a long time since he acted so irresponsibly. Coming of age had a way of bringing you to your senses. Facing a jail sentence had a way of doing it, too. He was lucky it never got to that point, thanks to his parents and some hard lessons learned. He only wished he had been the only one to pay for those lessons learned.

He drew in a frosty breath that chilled his lungs. Deep down he knew that everything he did was somehow connected to Chas and that fateful night. It had been a turning point for both of them. Unfortunately for Chas, Kyle had been the one to get the better end of the deal. If only they'd stayed put twelve years ago, Chas wouldn't have paid for his mistake.

Kyle grabbed a piece of fried dough from the concession stand and spied a St. Bernard leashed to a barrel marked "Non-perishable Food Donation." Immediately he thought of his dog, Max, lounging at home in front of the wood stove. At least, he hoped the dog was still lounging in front of the stove. After the Thanksgiving fiasco, both he and Max would be in the dog house if he wasn't. He didn't feel comfortable taking his dog to such a public affair. But giving it another thought, he wasn't sure leaving all one hundred and fifteen pounds of dog home alone with unprotected upholstery was a better alternative.

He patted the dog on the head and tossed a piece of fried dough, which the dog swallowed with one gulp.

The weather had been kinder tonight, rising a full ten degrees above what it had been hovering at for the last week. The sun had been out all day giving way to a beautiful star filled sky as a backdrop for the lighting of the sixty foot high Norwegian Pine tree in the center of the town common. He walked around. Looking. Searching.

He groaned inwardly. The Lauren Alexander thing was a dead issue. He'd thought about her all day and hoped she would come. He'd been through this crowd at least twice and still hadn't caught a glimpse of her and Kristen when he finally decided to head back to the concession stand for a cup of hot chocolate.

What was wrong with him? So she'd decided not to come, he fumed, jamming his free hand in his jacket pocket. It's not like she said she would. In fact, she flat out said she wouldn't. Still, he'd found himself hoping that she would change her mind.

Lauren walked the slippery sidewalk clutching Kristen's small mittened hand in hers. Her apartment was only a few short blocks from the town common.

Although the day had been warm and sunny, the temperature had dipped just below freezing after sunset creating a slick sheet of ice on the walkway. "Careful, Krissy," Lauren cautioned when she saw Kristen's feet slipping.

"I'm okay, Mommy," Kristen replied, looking up at her with a wide grin.

Kristen had heard about the tree lighting ceremony from the teacher at school today. When Lauren had picked her up from Mrs. Hopkin's apartment, Kristen talked endlessly about going. After the dinner dishes were finally cleared, washed and put away, she continued to express her desire to come and see Santa just one more time. In her heart, Lauren knew the reason. She wanted to ask Santa for a daddy again. In the end she conceded, bundling the two of them up for a cold Winter walk.

She really didn't want to go to this damned ceremony, Lauren kept trying to convince herself all day at work. She'd probably run into Kyle here and that was the last thing she needed. Images of Kyle Preston kept creeping back to her during the lull of phone calls that usually occupied her work day. The twinkle of glee in his eye as he stood beneath the lamppost and smiled at her, the well defined Nordic features of his face haunted her. This was not a good sign, she surmised. Yes, Kyle Preston was the last thing she needed in her life right now.

Why had she told him she was married? She recalled the conversation they'd had the previous evening when he helped her with her car and knew the reason. For the past seven years since Kristen's father left her alone and pregnant, she kept every prospective male suitor at arms length. Not that there were many, but her convenient declaration pretty much killed any and all prospective chances for romance.

Being married had been an excuse she used on numerous occasions while she was waitressing and encountered an over zealous, slightly intoxicated patron. Even some of the kitchen help that had asked her out for coffee after her shift were not immune to this excuse.

Yet with its convenience, it was still a lie. And Kyle had seen right through it where other men had simply accepted it as truth. But the truth was she was never married to Kristen's father. Her one and only sexual encounter that resulted in a teenage pregnancy, shattering her hopes and dreams for a promising future, had also shattered her first and only romantic relationship. Once Kristen was born, she kept her mind focused on raising the daughter she'd fought so hard to keep and pushed any notion of romantic entanglement aside. It had been easy for the past seven years. There really hadn't been anyone who'd turned her head and made her think of giving them half a chance. Until now.

"Hold my hand, honey," Lauren advised as they scurried across the busy intersection that led to the town common.

Although they had lived in town for the past six years, this was the first year they were coming out for the big festivities. Lauren had always worked nights as a waitress, choosing to spend her days at home with Kristen when she was a pre-schooler. Now that she had arrived and saw all the Christmas decorations and heard the carolers singing, she was just as excited as Kristen to be here.

"Did we miss Santa?" Kristen asked as she tugged on Lauren's arm, pulling her toward the decorated gazebo where Santa was expected to be seated.

Lauren took a quick look around. The tall pine tree had already been trimmed with a zillion lights waiting to be set ablaze. The long roped area off the front of the gazebo leading down toward the center of the tree lined common was already filled with parents and children waiting in line to tell Santa their Christmas wishes.

"We didn't miss anything, yet," Lauren confirmed. "Look, the tree is still dark. They wouldn't dare light the tree without Santa."

Kristen gave an excited squeal and wrenched at her mother's arm with impatience. "Come on, Mommy."

"Not yet, sweetie. Let me get a hot cup of something to drink first. It looks like they have some fried dough. Want some?" Lauren asked. It was the holiday season. The sugar coated dough was probably not the best thing for Kristen's teeth, but it was Christmas time. It was nothing an extra long brushing couldn't fix before climbing into bed.

"Yeah!" Kristen declared and began pulling her mother toward the concession stand.

That's when she saw Kyle talking to the woman behind the concession stand as he patted a gigantic dog tied to a barrel. Her first thought was to change directions and head toward the gazebo. Maybe she could get lost in the crowd. But she was too late. He swung around and saw her walking toward him, making no attempt to hide his surprise or pleasure at their arrival.

He stood up straight just staring at her with his cool as ice eyes, pushing the strands of hair the wind had blown in his face back with one brush of his hand. Even from the distance they were at she could tell he was a good ten inches taller than her five foot six frame. She noticed for the first time what she couldn't last night, he was exceedingly handsome. His hair was long, touching his shoulder blades in the back, with blonde tips and rich brown roots that gave it an almost frosted appearance. It was something she hadn't noticed last night when his hair was wet from the snow. His facial features were strong and hard, reminiscent of a Viking.

When he'd come out of nowhere last night and offered her aid, she'd feared him. She tried to tell herself it was because she was alone and he was a stranger. And now she feared him again, but it had nothing to do with her and Kristen's safety. It had everything to do with a need that had laid dormant inside her for far too long.

"I'm glad you made it," he said when they reached the concession stand. Lauren remained at a good ten foot distance, fearing the behemoth dog might leap on Kristen. "Oh, don't be frightened. They're big, but these dogs are pretty much harmless," Kyle assured them. "That is as long as you don't have any fried dough."

"Or a perfectly basted and stuffed turkey," the woman that Kyle had been conversing with spouted from behind the counter. Up close, Lauren guessed that she was no more than ten or fifteen years older than Kyle. She was petite in size and her short brown hair curled around her ear muffs. What she noticed more was the way her cocoa colored eyes gleamed with affection at Kyle, making Lauren wonder about the nature of their relationship. "A word of warning, my dear. Make sure you keep your hands and food held high."

Kyle laughed, but appeared slightly abashed. "Are you still sore about Thanksgiving, Ma?"

"What do you think?" the woman returned, rolling her eyes at Kyle.

"I think I'd better quit while I'm still ahead," he answered.

"Good thinking."

Kyle brushed his arm across Lauren's back and she immediately felt a pulse of warmth beneath her heavy coat from his touch. "Ma, this is Lauren Alexander and the little one hiding behind her here is Kristen."

Kristen shyly pulled into her mother in an attempt to hide herself. It was a typical reaction for Kristen when meeting new people. Of course, Kristen had no idea that she'd already met Kyle the previous evening and still felt intimidated.

"This is my mother, Judy Preston," he told Lauren.

"Nice to meet you Mrs. Preston," Lauren returned cordially. She held her gaze on Judy, noting her youthful appearance, then glanced back at Kyle as if to make the link. But she couldn't figure out what didn't seem right about the connection.

"Please call me Judy. Did you have any trouble finding a parking space? It gets so crowded and with all the snow, parking is scarce."

"We live just a few blocks from here so we walked," Lauren told her. "I had no idea this was such a big deal. We've never been."

"Really? You must be new to town. Brimfield has been putting on this celebration for years." Judy seemed nice and friendly, Lauren decided.

"We've lived here a few years. We just haven't had the opportunity to come."

"We're a rowdy crowd but we have a good time," Kyle said, giving her a mischievous grin.

Without warning, he placed his arm loosely around her shoulder. The gesture felt so natural that Lauren didn't think to pull away until it seemed it would become too obvious to everyone around them. Although the wave of heat his touch generated filled her with a stirring deep beneath the pit of her belly, she found herself enjoying the fire kindling inside her. It had been way too long since any man spawned such desires.

"So, Kyle tells me you're coming for dinner on Sunday," Judy said as if it were a confirmation of something already discussed.

"I beg your pardon?" Bewildered, Lauren looked, first at Judy, then at Kyle.

Kyle blew out a breath and gave her a crooked grin. "Ma, would you let me get around to asking her first?"

"What are you wasting time for? Just ask the girl, for cripes sake," Judy stated.

"Well, I, uh-" Lauren stammered.

"Are we going somewhere, Mommy?" Kristen asked curiously, looking up at Lauren with widened eyes.

"Here, have a cup of hot chocolate to warm you." Judy extended a styrofoam cup filled with hot chocolate and piece of fried dough lightly dusted with powdered sugar. Lauren automatically accepted, keeping the hot chocolate for herself and handing the pastry to Kristen.

Kyle quickly whisked her away from the concession stand. "Sorry about that."

"It's okay. She's just..." Lauren turned to look back at the concession stand, still reeling from the strange conversation.

"What is it?" he asked, answering her befuddled expression.

"I'm sorry. It was rude of me to stare. It's just that your mother..."

"I know. She spoke a little soon. But the invitation still stands. I mentioned to her this afternoon that I wanted to invite you and Kristen to dinner on Sunday. I hope you'll be able to make it," he said, squeezing Lauren's hand.

"No."

He stopped walking and jerked his body around to look at her. "You won't come for dinner?"

"No, that's not what I mean. It's just..." She didn't quite know how to verbalize her thoughts, especially since it was a cause of concern over being so young herself when Kristen was born. "Your mother seems so young." Heat filled her cheeks. It was a stupid thing to say, but honest none the less..

Kyle laughed. "She'd probably kiss you if she heard you say that."

"She seems too young to have a son your age is what I'm trying to say," she added.

"Most people pick up the fact that I tower over my parents or that they both have brown eyes and mine are blue."

Feeling embarrassed for such an inconsequential observation, Lauren crouched down to fiddle with Kristen's mittens that were now covered with powdered sugar from the fried dough.

As if sensing her discomfiture, he offered, "Mom and Dad knew early on they weren't going to have kids of their own. They adopted me."

"It's none of my business," Lauren blurted out, trying to brush off a flood of seven-year-old memories the word adoption evoked.

"It's okay. It doesn't bother me. It shouldn't bother you,"

Kyle returned as they made their way to the long line of people still waiting for Santa Claus to show.

"It doesn't," she stopped and turned to face him, trying her best not to appear frazzled. The last thing she wanted was for him to misread her hang-ups over adoption as being a negative reflection on him. The truth was, Lauren had never quite given up the guilt over almost giving Kristen up for adoption all those years ago.

"Really? Why do I get the feeling there is something more?" It was frightening, the way Kyle's eyes seared through her as if he was penetrating her soul, reading her deepest fear. No one had ever come close to doing that before.

She darted a quick glance at Kristen, then back to Kyle. A prickly heat scorched beneath her scarf and began to feel like a noose around her neck. His eyes softened and his expression fell as they took their place in the long line.

He opened his mouth to speak, but his voice was drowned out by the roar of the crowd as Santa Claus arrived on the back of a bright red fire engine. The truck drove around the common with lights flashing as Christmas carols blared on the loud speaker and scattered people lost in the crowd sang along to *Santa Claus is Coming to Town.* Lauren breathed a heavy sigh of relief for the distraction. She hadn't spoken a word of her guilt to anyone since the day she left the hospital with Kristen all those years ago. She'd be damned if she started now.

~3~

The flash of fear in Lauren's eyes startled Kyle. Her eyes were wide and luminous. It was many years ago, but he'd seen that same brand of fear before in Chas. Although a lot had changed since those rebel days, the memory of his friend's pain was etched in his brain forever.

And now he was seeing it again in Lauren. His first reaction was to reach out to her, hold her. Anything to erase that pain. But when he reached out to take her hand, she did something completely unexpected.

She laughed and shouted, "Come on!" Pulling both Kristen and Kyle deep into the crowd of people already joyfully caroling, she began singing at the top of her lungs. Kristen sang in between giggles and jumping up and down with glee.

A rush of excitement mixed with bewilderment consumed him. Was this the same woman who bluffed so miserably last night? Just when he thought he knew what to expect, she did a one hundred and eighty degree turn on him and raced in the other direction.

"You better watch out," she sang. "What's wrong? Join in," she urged.

They sang and laughed as Santa rode around the common

before making his way through the crowd of people. With the music still blaring over the loud speakers, she shouted, "It's a good thing they don't discriminate for singing out of tune."

His eyebrows furrowed. "Why's that?"

"Because you would have been kicked out of the choir long ago. You can't carry a tune to save your life." When she laughed, her voice was rich and pure and her face was bright, and happy.

His breath caught in his throat. "Hey, it's the enthusiasm behind the song that counts."

She nudged him. "If you say so."

As Santa Claus made his way through the cheering crowd, the town Christmas tree was set ablaze. A chorus of oh's and ah's filtered through the town square along with cheering.

Kyle gazed down at Lauren's face and was transfixed by the awe he saw there. Her mouth was open slightly and her eyes were wide with wonder. She stood with Kristen, staring up at the Christmas tree as if she'd never seen anything like it before. In fact, both mother and daughter looked as if they had just walked into Santa's winter wonderland with the golden key.

God, she was beautiful. He wanted to touch her, but didn't want to break the spell that had come over her.

They waited in line to see Santa, toes and noses frozen in the dipping temperature, watching the mist from their breath, without any real conversation. Despite the laughter they'd shared earlier, Kyle knew that there was something Lauren was holding back. She'd acted weird, to say the least, when she met his mom and he mentioned that he was adopted. Suddenly, he needed to know the reason why. Given the right moment, he fully intended to get to the bottom of what made Lauren Alexander so special.

"Look, the line has died down for sleigh rides. Why don't we take advantage of our luck?" Kyle said, gently tugging Lauren by the hand. It felt so natural holding her hand that when he realized he was doing it, he just held on and savored the toasty feeling it gave him.

"I really should get Kristen home," Lauren said. "She's been out late two nights in a row."

"It's not a school night. Surely, she doesn't have to be in bed so early," he challenged, hoping he could gain a little advantage by soliciting Kristen's help. He wasn't disappointed.

"Yeah, let's go see the horses!" Kristen squealed, scrunching her shoulders up to keep herself warm.

Lauren shot a you're-playing-dirty glance at Kyle and turned to Kristen. "But honey, you look so cold. I think we need-"

"We'll keep her warm. We can sit her between us," Kyle interjected before she could make another protest. Moving closer he added in a whisper, "Will that be a safe enough distance for you, Ms. Alexander?"

She sucked in a breath and peered straight into his eyes. He hadn't expected her to let go of his remark without a comeback. He figured she'd shoot back with that same wildcat fire he'd seen last night in the parking lot. What shocked him was seeing what washidden in the depths of her wide eyes. It looked almost like desire. And maybe a hint of fear. She said nothing and that surprised him most of all. But then again, he was finding out fast that Lauren Alexander was full of surprises.

"Thanks, Dad," Kyle said as the horse-drawn carriage came to a halt in front of one of the town's oldest Victorian homes, located just on the outskirts of the common. For the past three holiday seasons, his father had used two of the work horses from the farm to give sleigh rides on the back trails of the farm. But for use in the town square where the pavement was clear of snow, he needed the carriage to give "sleigh" rides.

"Anytime. We can take another ride after dinner on Sunday if you like," Will Preston said to Lauren as he helped her down from the sleigh. Kristen was still in her arms and well on her way to falling asleep. "We can take a real sleigh ride then. Maybe this little lady will stay awake to enjoy the ride next time." He smiled and rumpled the little girl's hair causing her to stir in Lauren's arms just enough to let out a lazy yawn.

"Well, I'm not sure that we can-"

"We better get Kristen inside," Kyle interrupted.

"Yes. It was nice meeting you, Mr. Preston."

"Likewise. Be seeing you on Sunday I'm sure," Will called out as he climbed back on to the carriage.

Kyle waved as his father rode away. "See you."

He grasped the cold brass knob and yanked the door with more force than a girl as tiny as Kristen could ever muster. "I'll be by tomorrow to oil this door. You're going to dislocate your shoulder if you keep this up."

"On the up side, I don't have to go to the gym. Thanks, but there's no need. Mrs. Hopkins' son usually comes by to do repairs when needed," Lauren said, dismissing his offer. Her hair shimmered in the moonlight giving her an angelic look that caught Kyle off guard. His eyes focused on the fullness of her glossy lips as he fought the urge to bend his head and steal a kiss. If it wasn't for Kristen being in her mother's arms, he probably would've done just that.

He wondered just what kind of man tosses aside a woman as beautiful as Lauren Alexander without any thought of the child they created. How that same man could live without the laughter just waiting to bubble up from the depths of her soul to fill his own. She was full of life just waiting to burst free. He'd seen just how much tonight when she pulled him into the crowd of Christmas carolers and sang to her heart's content.

"Let me take her," he offered, watching Lauren step awkwardly with a sleepy Kristen in her arms.

"No, thanks. I have her."

"It's a long way to the third floor."

"She's my daughter. I do it all the time." Lauren moved past him, her jaw squared and determined like she'd been last night, her boots scuffing against the worn wooden treads as she advanced up the stairs. He wondered if they'd ever get past this barrier. Tonight, he had hoped she'd lower her shield enough to let him get a real glimpse of her.

They climbed the three flights of stairs until they reached

the landing that headed to her attic apartment.

"Thank you once again, Kyle." She shifted Kristen in her arms and rattled her keys in her hand, but made no move to unlock the door. It was clear to him that she was debating whether or not to invite him in.

Without a word, he took the keys from her hand. "This one?" He lifted one of the keys for her to view.

She nodded. "There's a light switch on the left side as you open the door."

The door swung open and Kyle grazed his left hand against the smooth wall until he found the switch that illuminated the living room. He stepped in and Lauren breezed straight by him into a back room.

"I'll be out in a minute," she said in a voice just loud enough for Kyle to hear.

He pulled the key from the lock and closed the door behind him, jingling the keys in his hand as he scanned her home. It was a cozy attic apartment with slanted walls in the gable ends and old style woodwork that spoke of the craftsmanship of the building's earlier years. He brushed his hand over the stained wood in admiration. You didn't see moldings and cabinetry made with such detail in new construction. He'd have to remember the detail work when he added the finishing touches to his house.

As he walked into the open living room, his boot kicked something pliant, spilling its contents. He stooped to see the damage and found a wicker basket filled with magazines, some of which had scattered on the floor by the slipcovered sofa. He quickly refilled the basket with what would fit and placed the rest on the end table. He lingered a moment to read the cover of one of the magazines before placing it down next to a course catalog from a local community college.

The furniture, although worn from years of use, felt homey and invited you to sit down and get comfortable. Kyle guessed that everything was either a hand-me-down or bought at the Salvation Army store with limited funds. A picture frame perched on the television caught his attention. He picked up the wooden frame, a double oval containing a portrait of Lauren with a man and woman he guessed were her parents on one side, a candid shot of Kristen at the park in the other.

"She was asleep before I took her coat off. Didn't even stir." Lauren bounced into the room as if there had never been a moment of tension between them. Kyle leaned against a built-in bookcase and realized this was the first time he'd seen her without her bulky coat on. "Nice, isn't it?" she said.

"Hmmm. Oh, the woodwork? Yes, it's beautiful."

"It's one of the things I love about this apartment. Want some coffee? I have decaf."

"Yeah, sure."

She stretched to reach some mugs in a cabinet over the sink and he noticed that her long legs, accentuated by her form fitting jeans, were like that of a dancer's. They almost seemed too long for her torso. The coral turtleneck she wore tucked neatly into the waistband set off the color of her eyes and put a rosy glow on her creamy complexion.

She busied herself in the tiny, but functional kitchenette, seemingly unaware of Kyle's study of her. He had to admit he liked just gazing at her, the way she shuffled her socked feet on the floor, the way she unwittingly pushed her hair behind her ear to reveal the soft flesh of her earlobe.

"I hope you don't mind instant. As you can see, counter space is nearly nonexistent so there is no room for a coffee maker. Why don't you sit on the sofa and take off your coat? It's almost done. Oh, and how do you take your coffee?" she asked. Lauren knew she was babbling, but she couldn't help it. She always tripped over her own tongue when she was nervous. It was the first time she'd had a man who wasn't there to make repairs in her apartment. The first of many firsts, she guessed.

"Black, please."

With a trembling hand, she poured the boiling water into the two mugs, sloshing liquid over the brim of the second. She wiped up the spill with a dish towel and topped off her mug with milk before joining Kyle on the sofa.

This is so ridiculous. She was a grown woman acting like a school girl with her first crush. All she needed was pom-poms and a pony tail to complete the picture.

"Your family seems so nice," she commented. Anything to keep him from staring at her like he was about to swallow her whole. She wasn't sure if the thought frightened or excited her.

He smiled in response and his eyes lit up with such affection it made her heart ache.

"I noticed the pictures on the television." Kyle pointed to the picture frame.

"Krissy loves the jungle gym. She was just four years old then." Lauren clenched the hot mug in her hand and felt her sweaty palms burn against the ceramic.

"The couple with you, are they your parents?" he asked as he got up and retrieved the frame.

"Yes."

He sat down on the sofa next to her and smiled warmly as he stared at the faces behind the glass. "They must spoil Kristen rotten. Most grandparents do."

She dropped her mug on the table with more force than was necessary and regretted her gut reaction immediately. "She doesn't know them."

His expression fell and his eyebrows furrowed. "You don't see them?"

"No." She wasn't about to tell him it wasn't by her choice, but theirs. She couldn't stand the thought of his pity, nor did she welcome it.

"For God's sakes, why not?" He genuinely looked aghast. His clear blue eyes were darker in color, and his mouth agape.

"Not everyone has a close-knit family," she said softly, taking the frame from his hand and returning it to its rightful place.

She could feel his eyes probed her, seeking the answer to his questions. It made her insides churn.

"What could they have possibly done to make you leave?"

She straightened her spine and swung around to face him.

"It was a mutual thing, Kyle. I'd prefer not to dredge up the past. Can we talk about something else, please?"

He drew in a deep breath and for the first time Lauren saw the muscles of his chest expand against the hunter green cotton shirt he wore. He was strong in form where she had always considered herself strong in will. Why did the man make her insides crazy? She had an unfamiliar feeling of longing to touch him coupled with the terror of wanting to fly like a bat out of hell.

He smiled wickedly. "Okay, dinner on Sunday."

"What about it?" she asked as if she didn't already know what he was getting at.

"I've already spilled the beans and told my parents you were coming. To be perfectly honest, your presence there could help me redeem myself after the Thanksgiving fiasco."

She laughed, remembering Judy's mention of a perfectly basted turkey and decided to tease him. "Kyle, don't tell me you ate all the turkey. You're a grown man-"

"I wasn't the one who ate all the turkey. Anyway, you're never grown as far as your parents are concerned. Mine still think of me as the twelve year old dirty-faced kid that got deposited on their doorstep." His smile was wide and did wonders to help dissipate the tension caused by the mention of her parents.

Her mouth dropped open. "You were twelve?"

"Yeah. Here my folks were praying for a baby. You can imagine their surprise when all they got was a juvenile delinquent." He rubbed his face with his hand and shook his head as if in remembrance.

"I'm sure you weren't that bad or you wouldn't have ended up as successful as you are now," she suggested.

"Oh, success was a long time coming. The road getting to today has been pretty rocky." He dropped his gaze from her and circled the rim of his mug with the edge of his thumb.

"Tell me about it," she urged, suddenly intrigued.

He gave a quick smile. "Maybe some day."

"How am I going to help you redeem yourself if I don't know your story?"

"Does that mean you're coming?"

She'd backed herself into a corner with that one. "You know, I hadn't planned on going tonight. It was a spur of the moment decision. What would you have done if I hadn't shown up?"

He squinted one eye as he looked at her and said, "I probably would have been in the dog house."

"Why's that?"

"Let's just say that my mother is a maniac about three things-breakfast, lunch and dinner." He laughed hard and added, "And she doesn't share my need for taking in strays of the four legged variety."

"This sounds like a good story."

"Come on Sunday and I'll tell you about it."

She couldn't figure out why this meant so much to Kyle. But after meeting his folks, she had to admit the idea of a family Sunday sounded appealing. In fact, it seemed downright heavenly. She missed her own parents so much that she couldn't resist even a few hours in the company of nice people like the Prestons.

"We'll be there."

Lauren slammed the car door and stood in the driveway gazing at the Preston home. The house was something out of a Currier and Ives picture print. The lighted Christmas tree as well as the tiny white lights illuminating each window could be seen from the street and were the first thing to catch Lauren's attention. Snow clung to the evergreen garland strung around the railing and banister of the Farmers porch giving the house a welcoming quality.

With her gloved hand placed over her chest, she fought her emotions. It reminded her of her grandmother's home in upstate New York where she'd spent the holidays as a child.

She blew out a mist of breath. "They live in a postcard,"

Lauren muttered, unable to take her eyes from the picture perfect home.

"Mommy?" Kristen called from inside the car, breaking Lauren from her trance.

"Sorry, sweetie." She opened the door and helped Kristen out of the car, wondering if she would be able to make it through dinner without reliving all her childhood memories. Each Christmas Eve since she'd left home, she would cry for hours after Kristen was snug in her bed and the presents from Santa were neatly placed beneath the tree. Only she knew the heartache of what they were missing by being alone for the holidays.

The scent of pine needles intensified as they reached the front door. A wide wreath adorned with a bright red velvet bow hid most of the oval etched glass on the door. She rang the doorbell and immediately heard the scurry of feet and young voices running toward the foyer. Suddenly, she felt a mixed sense of excitement and apprehension fill her whole being. It was the kind of excitement she'd felt in her youth. Looking down at Kristen, she squeezed her little hand in hers and waited for the door to swing open.

"Hey," the young teenager said. Her hair was a multitude of color and shaved in various odd places. A quick glance at the line of shiny yellow studs in her ear made Lauren wonder if this girl had more gold than Fort Knox. "You Lauren?"

She nodded. "And this is Kristen," she said when the girl just stood there staring.

"Come on in."

From inside the foyer, Lauren was hit with the heavenly aroma of good old-fashioned home cooking. She missed that. Not that she was a bad chef, she just hadn't quite mastered much beyond a can of soup and a box of macaroni and cheese. It was a good thing Kristen wasn't finicky.

"Kyle!" the girl called out. Turning to Lauren, she added, "He's in the family room, wrestling with Scotty."

Judy appeared in the foyer wiping her hands on her apron

before holding her hands out to take Lauren and Kristen's coats. "You don't have to scream to the whole neighborhood, Zoey," she said to the teenager. She turned to Lauren and said, "I'm so glad you made it. I hope you didn't have any trouble finding the house."

"No, I drive right by your house on the way to work, so I knew how to come."

Lauren sensed Kristen's apprehension and drew her close. It wasn't often that they dined at a stranger's home. But Lauren noticed her eyes light up and she beamed when she saw a little girl with carrot red hair, about the same age as Kristen, come romping down the stairs. Immediately, Lauren noted the little girl's distinctive features did not resemble any of the other members of the family and knew she must also be adopted.

"Julie!" Kristen squealed. In the next few minutes, they all learned that Julie, Judy's daughter, was a classmate of Kristen's. The two friends bolted upstairs to play with a doll house in Julie's room.

Suddenly feeling alone, Lauren took a deep breath and followed Judy down the hallway to a room off the back of the large eat-in kitchen. When she saw a long blond form stretch out on the floor being tackled by a child dressed in a Batman costume, Lauren realized it must be Kyle. A chuckle bubbled up from inside her and she placed her hand over her mouth to muffle her laughter.

"Lauren's here," Judy announced. "And don't you dare hurt your brother."

Kyle twisted around until he saw Lauren. His face was red and his hair tousled from rough housing with the little boy. "Okay, Scotty, you won."

The little caped crusader wound up his fist and slugged Kyle in the stomach.

"Ooof! I said you won, buddy." Kyle rubbed his stomach and shook his head as he lifted to a kneeling position. "That little guy packs a pretty good punch," he said to Judy. "And you were afraid that I was going to hurt *him*?"

Judy playfully smacked him on the back of his head with her hand. "Oh, don't be such a baby. Dinner will be ready in about a half hour or so."

"It's a good time to feed Max. Care to brave meeting man's best friend?" Kyle asked, now standing. "I'll tell you all about Thanksgiving."

"Don't remind me," Judy said as she left the room.

He laughed. "Come on. I'll show you around."

Kyle clamped the collar of his coat as he and Lauren walked the frozen pebble stoned path toward the carriage house. He shot a quick glance over to Lauren as she walked beside him. The moon light created a sheen against her silky blond hair that gave a sultry quality to the soft features of her face. She turned and caught him staring and dipped her head in response before returning a coy smile. My, but she was pretty.

Tonight, she had a particularly noticeable bounce in her step as they walked and he wondered why? Hopefully, it was because she was having a good time, he thought. The way he'd commandeered her into coming to dinner may not have been the smoothest way to approach the woman, but it had been effective just the same.

"I didn't realize that your sister Julie was in Kristen's class," Lauren said.

"Julie is so shy. I'm glad she's taken to Kristen. They'll have a good time together today."

Lauren chuckled. "All Julie had to say was the word 'doll house' and Krissy flew up the stairs."

"Does she have one?"

"No, but I know she'd love one. What little girl wouldn't?"

"Is Santa bringing her one?" Kyle said, giving her a wink.

He watched her expression droop, but she still held on to her smile. "Not this year. Santa's budget is not quite that big."

Kyle stopped walking when they got to the side door of the carriage house that led to his apartment and he paused. His first thought was that if Lauren was in need, he'd just loan her the money. He knew that she had a hard time accepting help from others, so giving her money as a gift would certainly be out of the question. Money had ceased to be an issue for him since his explosion into the world of real estate development, but the last thing he wanted to do was insult Lauren with an offer of charity.

With full force, he pulled open the sliding door, flicked the light switch on the wall, and waited until Lauren walked into the garage section of the carriage house. He steered her to a closed set of stairs that rose to the living quarters.

"I could get her one," he suggested as they climbed the stairs, going against his earlier reasoning.

Lauren swung around to face him straight on, her mouth agape and her eyes widened. "Certainly not."

"Why not? It'll be a gift from Santa."

"It would be a gift from you. Look, I appreciate the offer, but there are lots of things Kristen wants that she doesn't get. It's not like she could possibly get everything on her Christmas list." Lauren took a deep breath and rolled her eyes. "What list? All she asked for was a daddy and she's not going to get that, either."

She turned and climbed the stairs until she reached the top landing. Kyle noticed the sudden heaviness in her step and regretted bringing up a subject that had caused her unrest.

Her smile had been so bright when she walked into the family room, almost as bright as when the town Christmas tree was set ablaze. He wondered what she had been thinking to make her expression so radiant. But now, she seemed as down as she had the first night they met and it was eating at his insides.

Kyle opened the door a crack, then pulled back after he heard the heavy thump of a charging dog on the other end. "Better let me go first. This dog...well...Max is kind of mammoth," he warned.

As usual, Max met Kyle at the door with slobbering licks, a heavy tail wag that could knock out a cow, and repeated gnawing on the sleeve of his coat to get his undivided attention.

"You weren't kidding, he's big!" Lauren gasped.

"Down, Max." The dog continued jumping. "I said down!" Kyle commanded in a deep authoritative voice.

Lauren kept her distance. "Have you had him long?"

"He's a stray. I've only had him a few weeks." He picked up one of his old running shoes that Max had apparently used as an afternoon snack. "As you can see, he's not exactly trained. Okay, boy, what else did you eat?"

Kyle looked around and assessed the damage while filling the dog's dish with food and water. Thinking it was safer all around to let him out, he put the dog in the side yard on a run while Lauren stayed in the apartment. When
he returned, Lauren had her coat off and was seated at the pedestal kitchen table reviewing a set of blueprints he'd left out earlier. His footsteps startled her. She darted a glance up at him like a child with her hand caught in the cookie jar and carefully placed the blueprints back on the table.

"I'm surprised Max didn't eat them," Kyle said. "What do you think?"

"Of...the blueprints?"

"Yeah."

"It's a beautiful house."

He smiled with pride. "I could take you by to see it some time."

Her eyes widened. "You mean...it's yours?"

"Yes. I have a twenty acre lot over on Tower Hill Road. It's still under construction, but it's close to being completed." Well, that was true enough, he thought. He'd been working on the house for the past two years, making so many changes that he thought he'd never finish. In a way, the thought of the project coming to an end depressed the hell out of him. What was he going to do in a big house all alone? That wasn't the way it was supposed to be when he started the project.

Lauren picked up the plans and began studying them.

"I've put a line of full view windows off the family room," he said, pointing to the blueprints. "There's a great view of the hills from the back of the property. A nice flat backyard that goes back a ways before it drops."

"Nice for kids," she noted.

"That was the idea. I'd hoped to have a few."

She lifted her head from the blueprint and quirked an eyebrow.

"I had been seeing someone for a while when I decided to build the house," he informed her, recalling that it had been Debra who'd actually pressed him to build a house of their own. He would have preferred staying in the carriage house until they decided to start a family. But Debra insisted she'd feel too "confined" and wanted something of her own.

"So the house was for you and her?"

He nodded. "I was too deep into construction to stop the project when the relationship ended, so I'm finishing it."

"It's a little big for one person."

His sentiment exactly. "I've been thinking of putting it on the market when it's complete."

Lauren studied the plans again. "I noticed you put walls in the dining room. You should've knocked them down on both sides to open it up. Makes it more inviting. It's hard to move around in a house filled with family and friends during the holidays when..." Her voice trailed off and she blinked as if she were trying to force something out of her mind.

"This place is like a zoo during the holidays," he said softly. "But I wouldn't have it any other way. How about you?"

Her expression drooped again and he silently cursed himself for being the cause.

"We used to go to my grandmother's house for Christmas every year." Her full lips lifted to a smile, but Kyle noticed a hint of melancholy with her remembrance. "I used to think it was a drag to drive all the way upstate just for the day when I was a kid, but I always loved it." She blinked again, hard this time, and Kyle knew that she was holding back tears.

"Kristen must love it. Most little kids do."

"Kristen has never been. We stopped going when..." She shrugged and bit her bottom lip.

Well, at least that explained the tears and the strong feeling of independence. "When you left your parents," he finished.

"I didn't leave them. They sent me away." She stood up and fiddled with a lock of hair behind her ear.

He felt her pain as his own like a stab in the gut. It was the same pain he'd felt long ago standing in that courtroom listening to his father's rejection. "I'm sorry," he said, knowing his words sounded feeble at best.

She looked up at him and he saw a single tear run down the side of her cheek. He cupped that cheek with his hand and brushed the moisture away with his thumb. Her skin was silky and warm and Kyle knew without a doubt that he'd never felt so dizzy just being this close to a woman before. But Lauren Alexander wasn't just any woman.

"Will you tell me what happened?"

He expected her to swing around and give him the standard, "It's none of your business" routine, but her eyes held a heaviness that told him she needed to unload her feelings. He guessed that maybe it was burden she'd held far too long.

~4~

Lauren felt the muscles in her throat tighten. That damned noose! Pulling on the collar of her royal blue turtleneck, she walked to the beige leather sofa in the center of the living room. But she didn't sit down. Her nerves skittered through her veins as her mind raced.

The room, Kyle's home, felt warm and cozy despite being so large. The living room was square and wide open with a cathedral ceiling boasting wooden planks that soared towards the apex of the room. It was quite a contrast to the slanted walls of her attic apartment. On the far end of the room was an oversized bay window that looked out to the backyard of the main home. An antique pool table stood in front of the window. Along the wall sat a stereo cabinet with CDs scattered about and a large screen television. Although it looked like a picture torn from the pages of Macy's furniture catalog, it lacked any kind of detail. The detail that a woman brings to a home, Lauren decided. It had her wondering about the women who had spent time here in Kyle's home, his bed.

She shook the thought aside. As abrasive as the thought was, it wasn't any of her concern, she told herself. Why should she care how many women had hung their panties on Kyle

Preston's bedpost?

"There's really not much to tell," she murmured, nervously brushing her hand against her other arm. The words of untruth left a bitter taste in her mouth. There was a whole lot to tell, she just didn't know if she could do it without breaking down for the umpteenth time.

"If that were the case, you wouldn't be avoiding it."

"I'm not avoiding anything, Kyle," she countered. "I just don't see any point in rehashing something that can't be changed. It's not worth it."

She heard him draw a deep breath. "It's at least worth a try."

Squeezing her eyes shut, she fought the threat of burning tears and desperately tried to keep her breathing even. "You don't understand."

"But I want to," he said softly. The deep timbre of his voice felt like gentle fingers caressing her soul.

She swung around to meet his gaze and found nothing but warmth and compassion. "I upset the apple cart by marring their perfect family image."

He made no move to come closer to her. The distance felt safe. But at the same time, it also felt lonely. So many times she had cried without any arms to hold her. The idea of Kyle's arms wrapped tight around her now seemed comforting, inviting.

He said nothing, but sat straddling a kitchen chair, resting his arms over the back.

She drew in a deep breath for courage, for strength, but could find none. "They had very high expectations for me. So did I," she continued.

"Most parents do."

"My parents aren't *most* parents." She pushed a lock of hair behind her ear and fiddled with its end, twisting it nervously between her thumb and her index finger. "I was going to be an architect."

He nodded his head. "I remember seeing a copy of *Architectural Digest* in your apartment the other night."

She gave a weak smile. "Well, maybe someday. Anyway, I was the kind of kid who did everything that was expected of me because it was expected. You know, the perfect Honor Society student, the devoted and obedient daughter. I was so *predictable.* My parents are psychologists, very well respected members of the community."

"Sounds like something to be proud of."

"Yes, it is, until your only daughter suddenly becomes unpredictable and starts dating a boy you don't approve of, someone who is nothing but trouble. Except I didn't see Jimmy as trouble then. I saw him as the Prince Charming who finally noticed the mousy, shy me that none of the other boys noticed."

He gave a lopsided grin. "I doubt that."

"You didn't know me back then. I admit I was taken with the attention Jimmy showered on me. I ignored all the things people told me about how he was no good, that he'd never change." She saw him flinch, and her heart sank. Would he judge her for her past? "But it was all true, only the truth came too late for me."

"I can see how a parent would have a problem with their daughter dating someone who was trouble," he said in a low voice. "But that's no reason to break all ties with your family."

"You don't know the half of it." She bit her bottom lip before going on. "I don't know what they were more upset about, my jeopardizing a promising future by getting pregnant or having everyone in the community watch their pregnant daughter hobble across a stage to collect her High School diploma." Sadly, she always believed it was the latter. How else could it explain her father's reaction when she told him she wanted to keep her baby? How else would it explain the tension that continued to keep them apart now?

That day. That God awful morning she sat waiting in her hospital room, just two days after Kristen was born. Waiting for her parents to come and take her home. Waiting for the nightmare to finally be over. The nurse came into her room repeatedly and asked her if she wanted anything for the pain. But she just said no. Nothing she could give her would make the pain in her empty arms go away.

She wasn't allowed to be in the maternity ward. It was better that way, easier for everyone involved, she was told. Easier for who? Lauren cried. Certainly not her. But everyone decided it was best to give the baby up for adoption. Lauren would go away to college, just as planned.

When she graduated and became a successful architect, her parents would eventually get over the "scandal" and everything would get back to normal.

Except nothing was normal. After tossing in bed for hours the night before, she did the unspeakable. She crept up to the maternity ward in the middle of the night and peeked through the wide glass window of the nursery to see the baby, her baby, wailing at the top of her lungs.

Her daughter was alone, all alone in a bassinet in the middle of the room with no one to comfort her. What was wrong with them? Why wasn't anyone taking care of her child? Lauren fumed. Why didn't anyone tell me my baby needed me?

Acting on pure instinct, she stormed into the nursery and scooped the baby into her arms. Kristen, so soft and warm, calmed down immediately and peered up at her mother with wonder shining in her wide eyes. It was then that Lauren understood the true meaning of unconditional love.

But then the head nurse snatched Kristen from her arms and ordered her to leave. Another nurse called a security guard and Lauren was hauled away in tears. She tried to tell them it was her baby, but they wouldn't listen. She couldn't see her baby. It was not allowed. She thought she'd died that night.

When her parents finally arrived with a lawyer to have her sign the adoption papers, she couldn't tell them what she'd done. They said they'd stand by her no matter what, and they had. They supported her when she decided against having an abortion and when Jimmy disappeared from her life.

They endured the pain with her when people stared and snickered about how their perfect family wasn't so perfect anymore. Surely they wouldn't desert her if she told them she couldn't give her baby away to strangers.

In the last second, when the lawyer put the adoption papers in front of her and asked her to sign her rights away, Lauren defied them. Twisting the pen between her fingers, she stared at the blank line marked with an X for what seemed an eternity. In the end, she knew there was no easy way to tell them that all she wanted to do was hold her baby.

"Everyone makes mistakes, Lauren. It was a long time ago," Kyle said.

"Yes, it was. And I don't regret any of the mistakes I've made because, if I did, it would mean that Kristen wouldn't be in my life. And I can't imagine that. But it doesn't change anything. I disappointed them and they've never forgiven me for it."

"How do you know that? Have you tried to contact them?"

"Yes. I send them birthday and Christmas cards and anniversary cards. I call them every year during the holidays, hoping they'll want to see me. But it's always so awful. Dad won't come to the phone, and Mom rushes me off because we don't know what to say to each other. They know where I am. But they've never made any move to contact me on their own." She swallowed hard, but the lump in her throat would not ease. "They've never seen Kristen. They left the hospital without even looking at her. They told me they wouldn't support me and they meant it."

"What did you do? Where did you go?"

She shrugged. "I managed. I had some money saved for college, so I bundled Kristen up and got on a bus. I knew the money wouldn't last, but I stretched it out long enough to move here and get a job waitressing at a good restaurant. I did that until this past September when Kristen started school. Part of me hoped that I'd be able take some classes and get my degree."

He smiled. "I'm sure you will someday."

She tried to smile, but the muscles in her face wouldn't cooperate. All her childhood dreams seemed a million miles away. "I barely have time to brush my teeth, Kyle. Did you forget I have a six year - old?"

He lifted himself from the chair and dragged it to the table before absorbing the distance between them. Though they weren't touching, she could feel his warmth. "Things change, Lauren. People *can* change."

She laughed sardonically. "You really believe that?"

Nodding his head, he said, "You should, too."

She shook her head. "It's a nice fairy tale."

"Give them a chance. Tell them you want to see them," Kyle urged.

She sighed as she walked over to the table and picked up her coat. "It must be time for dinner," she said, moving toward the door.

"You need to try again. You owe it to yourself and-"

She cut him off before he could finish. "We'd better get back to the house. Kristen will wonder where I am."

Kyle pushed his plate away and stared at Lauren sitting across from him at the antique table. Although she smiled pleasantly and engaged in small talk with his family, he knew it was just a front. All during dinner, he watched as she picked at her food and twisted her fork without so much as taking a bite.

"Did you see my new earring, Kyle? This makes ten," Zoey said, pulling at her gold clad earlobe.

Groaning, Kyle inspected the stud his sister had added to her collection. "At least it goes with all the colors of your hair, Zoey."

She waved him off and huffed. "I should have known you'd have no taste in fashion. You like it Lauren, don't you?"

"Uh, sure. Very nice," Lauren complemented. She looked at Kyle and shrugged.

Turning her attention to Judy, Zoey added with excitement, "Bruce says he's gonna get me one for my nose and my belly button for Christmas."

Kyle darted a glance over at his father, who sat at the head of the mahogany table with his arms knotted across his chest and his eyebrows raised as high as his skin could stretch. Patience and tolerance were Will Preston's strong suits, but Kyle could tell his father was just about ready to blow it.

"How, ah, nice, Bruce," Judy replied with forced graciousness. "Very...thoughtful."

Zoey smiled at Kyle, then leaned into her boyfriend, who had yet to crack a smile or say one word during dinner, and snaked her arm around his waist.

It made Bruce blush.

It made Kyle nauseous.

"How wonderful. And this you do...why?" Kyle finally asked because no one else dared.

"Oh, I can't talk to you, Kyle." Zoey stood up and started to clear the dirty dishes from the table. "Mom, is it okay if me and Bruce skip dessert? We're gonna catch an early movie."

"Sure, just be home by nine."

"How about eleven," Zoey bargained. "The movie gets out at nine and we thought we'd get a pizza or something-"

"You've got school tomorrow," Will interjected. "Be home by nine-thirty."

"Awe, Dad. Ten-thirty."

"You're sixteen years old, young lady. The curfew still stands."

"Max and I will hunt you down," Kyle cut in teasingly. Although he smiled, he kept his eyes fixed on Bruce. What his sister ever saw in this guy, or the portfolio of tattoos he displayed, was beyond him. The best thing he could say about them dating was that their hair colors matched.

"Stay out of this, Kyle," Zoey shot back.

Being the peacemaker of the family, Judy clapped her hands together and cut in with her usual flair, before war erupted.

"I have a cheesecake for dessert. I hope everyone left room for some," she said. Lauren stood up and started helping, but Judy held up her hand. "No, no. You just sit here and relax. I can take care of it. Zoey, will you help me with the coffee before you leave?"

The little ones excused themselves and scooted into the family room to watch a video.

Bruce bounded from the table and exited the room with Zoey. Both Kyle and Will dropped their heads forward in disgust.

"I don't know what the heck I'm going to do with that one." Will rubbed his face with both his hands and looked up at the ceiling. "Please, Lord, tell me she'll outgrow him."

Zoey swung through the doorway, her Army coat draped over one hand, a tray with plates topped with cheesecake in the other. She deposited the tray on the center of the table and rushed to kiss Will on the cheek. "See you, Dad."

"Remember what I said. Nine-thirty on the nose." She rushed out of the dining room and he added under his breath, "Or I'll take Max and hunt you down."

Kyle chuckled and looked across the table at Lauren. She shifted nervously in her seat, seemingly uncomfortable with the conversation. He wondered if she was thinking of herself at that age. Of her own parents' disapproval. Hard as he tried, he couldn't imagine her dating someone even remotely like Bruce.

A scuffling noise erupted from the kitchen that sounded like scratching paws on the tile floor. He heard the familiar bark. "Oh, no," Kyle groaned as he bolted to a stand.

"Whoa! Incoming!" Zoey called from the other room.

"Kyle Preston!" Judy screamed.

As if on cue, Will dove to the center of the table and grabbed the cheesecake tray just as Max pounced into the dining room. Kyle chased the dog around the table unsuccessfully until the animal lunged on top of the table, sniffing and slobbering for tidbits. Lauren jumped from her seat and stepped away from the table, her hand to her chest.

"I got him, Ma," Kyle said to Judy when she appeared in the doorway, hands on hips and scowling. To Lauren he said, "In case you were still wondering, this is what happened on Thanksgiving."

Judy's lips were tight. "Except that time this...this..."

"Max," Kyle offered.

"This *animal* got away with the turkey and dragged it through my house." Her nostrils flared with anger.

Will cleared his throat and eyed Kyle in a message that said he'd better take care of Max before the woman of the house did.

"Come on, boy." Kyle clutched the dog by the chewed leash and yanked, while Max continued to sniff for leftovers on the floor. When he got to the doorway, Judy glared at him and stepped back to let them pass. Kyle shrugged and said quietly, "Sorry, Ma."

"Oh, go. I swear, Kyle Preston, you get worse as you get older. You don't have to take in every stray that wags its tail on your doorstep," he heard his mother say as the kitchen door slammed shut.

As he crossed the driveway, he saw the red taillights of a car exiting the driveway. "I hope she knows what she is doing, Max," he said to the dog. Max whined, pulling away until Kyle ground his feet in to keep standing.

He let the dog pull him to the back of the carriage house and noticed the frayed end of the leash where Max had broken free. "Looks like I'm going shopping first thing in the morning for a strong chain," he muttererd to himself.

He deposited the dog in his apartment, saying a silent prayer that his home would remain in relative order while he was gone.

Pushing the kitchen door of his parents' home closed, he heard the sound of laughter spilling from the dining-room. Lauren's laughter. God, what a beautiful sound. "He was a lot of trouble? I can't imagine it." Lauren's wide eyes twinkled with delight as she watched him sink into the dining room chair.

"Don't let him fool you. Kyle wrote the book on trouble." Judy handed him a plate of cheesecake. But given the current topic of conversation, he didn't feel much like eating. "Kyle and Chas, I should say. The two of them were notorious for getting into everything."

"Really?" Lauren stared at Kyle in disbelief. Well, he never meant to paint himself as anything other than what he was, but he didn't go broadcasting his youthful indiscretions.

"There was the time you and Chas rolled that gigantic tractor tire down Main Street and wedged it in front of the Town Hall doors. I still can't believe no one saw you two do that," Will said, shaking his head.

"Or," Judy eyed Kyle, this time with affection, "the time you two *borrowed* Mr. Marsh's horse and strung it up on the water tower for the whole town to see."

Lauren's eyes flew open. "You put a horse on a tower?" she gasped.

Kyle shrugged uneasily. "It was a life-size plastic horse from the dairy over on Mill Brook Road. You know the one displayed at the front gate?"

Lauren nodded. "Oh, my word. How did you get that thing up the tower?"

"He used the Romex wire from my van." Will chuckled. "I got to Mrs. McAffree's house bright and early the next morning to re-wire her house with no wire for the job. And of course, there was the time-"

Kyle cleared his throat and extended his cup. "How about some coffee, Ma?" he asked as Judy refilled Lauren's cup. She turned and filled the cup he held out to her.

"Speaking of Chas, he called earlier today when you were out," Judy mentioned matter of factly. "Seems he and Kim are coming back to Palmer. Things didn't work out like he'd planned in New Jersey so they decided to come back here before Kim has the baby."

"Really?" he answered. "That's too bad. It'll be good to see him again, though."

"I invited him Christmas Eve. You and Kristen are welcome, too, Lauren. Unless, of course, you'll be with your family."

Lauren's face showed a trace of her plummetting spirits.

"Great idea," Kyle broke in before she could answer. "What do you say?"

"Well, I, ah..." she stammered.

"No need to decide right now. You let Kyle know. He'll be ho-hoing for the kids again this year."

Kyle half grinned. "Max can be my reindeer."

"He'll be no such thing. That dog is so far from my good graces, I don't want him in my house."

Kristen and Julie ran into the room with Scotty on their tails. "He wants to shoot us!" Kristen screamed.

"Yeah! With the gun!" Julie confirmed. Then the girls giggled as they climbed into their mothers' arms.

"Scott William Preston," Will scolded as the little boy ran around the dining room table sporting a plastic gun loaded with a sponge torpedo on the end. "You know better than to scare the girls."

When Scotty ran around the table, Kyle hooked him with his arm and reeled him in, tickling him as he squirmed on his lap.

Lauren chuckled softly, her head still spinning from the chatter during dinner, trying to keep track of all the conversations going on at once. It was a crazy arena. Being an only child, it was something she never understood. She marveled that no one else here seemed to have any trouble keeping it all straight. But then again, it was probably second nature to them.

Watching the commotion around her, she noticed how Kristen interacted and thrived among Kyle's family. The outgoing personality and confidence her daughter displayed both filled her with pride and stabbed at her heart.

Involuntarily, she clutched her stomach and felt it tighten with the thought of how their lives could have been. If Kristen had been adopted, she would have had a family like this. She would have had Sunday dinners and maybe even sisters and brothers like Julie and Scotty. Had she been selfish to only think of what she was losing by giving Kristen up for adoption? She never once thought of what Kristen would be missing in her life. Never.

And now Kristen wanted a daddy. What else did she want that Lauren couldn't provide?

Everyone around her moved in slow motion. She looked at the faces, smiling, laughing, joking, as if she were in suspended animation. It suddenly seemed surreal.

Someone touched her shoulder and she jumped. She looked

up into Kyle's smiling eyes. The lines she'd seen around his eyes earlier had smoothed. She touched his hand and felt her heart race. It wasn't just Kristen who needed something more in her life. Deep down, Lauren knew she'd gone far too long with her own unfulfilled needs.

And Kyle Preston was just the kind of man to satisfy those needs. But at what price, and for how long?

A short time later, Lauren thanked Judy for the lovely dinner and sent Kristen up to Julie's room to help clean up the toys.

She waited in the foyer, her wool coat draped over her arm. Kyle leaned against the doorjamb staring at her, looking through her, and making her incredibly nervous.

"What's going on in that head of yours?" he asked.

"I'm not sure I know what you're talking about." She avoided his gaze by looking at the pattern of the marble floor.

He reached forward and brushed in his fingers across her cheek. But she didn't look at him, couldn't look at him. "Yes you do," he said in a whisper.

"Am I still that predictable?"

"Anything but." The rough timbre of his voice caused her to finally look up at him. He sucked in a deep breath of air, expanding his chest against the cotton shirt he wore.

He was strong, no doubt about it. He had a strength she longed to wrap herself around, but feared like nothing before. She had the distinct feeling it wouldn't take much for her to tangle herself in his hold.

He bent his head closer to hers and said, "I can't figure you out."

"I'm...not all that complicated."

He laughed softly. "You look at me like you do, but you don't want to get involved," he said as he cupped both of her cheeks in his palms, forcing her to finally gaze up into his eyes. "That complicates things."

She closed her eyes and swallowed. The startling reality shocked her to her senses. It wasn't fear that seized her, it was desire. And damn, he knew it. "Kyle, please..."

"Look at me."

She didn't move. She heard his shallow breathing echo in her ear louder and stronger than the sounds of laughter upstairs from the children and the clanging of dishes and pans from the kitchen.

"Are you afraid of what you'll see? Of what I'll do?" he murmured when she didn't answer.

No, she thought, I'm afraid of what you'll see written all over my face.

This has to stop. She had to end it right here and now if she had any chance at all of getting away from Kyle Preston and the magnetic hold that was drawing her to him.

She shook her head and his hands fell away from her, leaving her cold. Straightening her spine, she took a stand.

"I'm sorry if I've been sending you mixed signals, but...you're right. I don't want to get involved. I don't intend to start something that I have no intention of finishing."

"No one is defining anything yet. We can take things as fast or as slow as you want."

"I don't want to take things at all."

"I don't understand."

"My daughter is very sensitive. She has hopes for a daddy for Christmas. I can't have men coming into Kristen's life today, giving her false hopes that they'll be around tomorrow."

"What makes you think I won't be around tomorrow?"

She blinked hard. "It's not fair to her."

He looked away as if she'd slapped him. "Are you sure that it's really your daughter you're trying to protect?"

She cleared her throat. "Yes. I hope I've made my position clear."

His jaw squared as his gaze seemed to bore into her soul. "Perfectly."

~5~

Monday morning turned out better than Kyle had anticipated. After getting too little sleep the night before, he downed a cup of black coffee and made a quick call to the newspaper. Three weeks of ads running in the paper and still no one had claimed ownership of Max. He swung around to the vet to give Max a checkup and make sure he had all the required shots before stopping by the house to do some work.

Inhaling a breath of clean winter air, Kyle looked out on the mountain view in the back of the property. A snowshoe rabbit poked its head out from underneath a broken pine limb before hiding again. Max darted his ears up and wiggled his nose, but couldn't find the little creature before it disappeared from sight.

It had been at least a month since he'd been out to the construction site. He'd forgotten just how much he loved this place.

The only thing he didn't like about it was the idea of living here alone. He'd spent too much time bucking family members and rejecting the love that was given him, that when he finally knew it, felt it, he didn't want to give it up.

With thoughts of Lauren, he rubbed his chest where he felt an ache and gazed out at the thick blanket of smooth snow covering the ground. Except for the deer tracks he spotted out back, the whole yard was as smooth as a baby's bottom, thanks to last nights snowfall. Reaching back, he picked up a piece of scrap wood from the barrel on the cedar deck just off the back of the house and pitched it out to the yard. Max flew from the deck and quickly clambered after it, tramping through the snow like a big floppy slipper, burying himself until he found the scrap.

Scotty and Julie always enjoyed coming out here to sled down the slope out back. Now there was a fresh coat of snow to cut through. Maybe this weekend, he mused.

Kyle let out a shrieking whistle to Max, but was not at all surprised when the dog didn't respond. He chased after the dog, rolling in the snow and getting himself wet in the process, until he got him on the new chain he'd purchased.

After pulling a few logs from the pile out back, he set a fire in the wood stove in the den. Since the house was still unoccupied, there was no sense running the heating system. He'd always used electric space heaters when he was working if it got too cold, but he couldn't use them today for what he planned to do.

He tossed his ski jacket to the kitchen counter and pushed up the sleeves of his UMass Amherst sweat shirt. Standing in the dining room, he looked long and hard at the walls on either side of the room. "Well, Preston, I hope you know what you're doing," he said to himself.

Funny how he was so sure of himself when it came to dealing with business. Put him in front of Lauren Alexander and he felt like he couldn't even recite the alphabet.

He'd been lucky enough to be at the right place at the right time during his business career and take advantage of many win-win situations. After countless business deals and property renovations where the name of the game was money, he had to wonder what else was in store for his life. Money didn't keep him warm at night when he was sleeping in a cold bed. Finally being at a point in his life where he had much to share, he had no one to share all that he'd achieved with.

And then he'd met Debra three years ago. At first, everything was great. With her being the youngest of eight children, Kyle had foolishly thought that family was an important part of her life and she understood how much it meant to him. But he was wrong. What meant a lot to Debra was how much Kyle could give her. Period. Like many of the women he'd dated once he'd become successful in business, she was attracted to his checkbook. When it became obvious that she resented the time and attention he gave his family, their relationship crumbled. But not before he was deep into constructing the house Debra had wanted so much. His enthusiasm for the project plummeted soon after.

But Lauren wasn't like that. She was fiercely independent, devoted to Kristen and...stubborn...and incredibly beautiful. Since they'd met, Kyle was beginning to think that maybe she was someone he could share his life with, too. Maybe he wouldn't be living here alone after all. The way she'd opened up to him about her parents, seeing the way she had blended right in with his family, he thought she'd finally started to lay down the shield she used to guard herself. Despite the rift that tore her family apart, Lauren didn't seem like the kind of woman who'd reject family without a reason.

But then she did a complete about face on him when she left. The Lauren who'd sat at the dining room table, laughing and listening to stories turned into another person. Her words were like a whip to his back.

I can't have men coming into Kristen's life today, giving her false hopes that they'll be around tomorrow. Like Debra, did Lauren not want to be part of a family? Was that the real reason she'd drifted away from her own?

Max barked out back just as Kyle heard the familiar sound of a van pulling into the driveway out front. A few minutes later, he heard a toolbox thump on the front porch and the thud of boots kicking against the sill.

"Thanks for swinging by on such short notice, Dad," he said when Will walked into the house.

"Having an electrician as a father certainly has its perks." Will looked around the room and nodded his head toward the wood stove. "No electricity? Is there a problem with the outlets?" He flipped a few switches as he walked around the room.

"No, I shut down the panel." Kyle placed his hand on the dining room wall adjacent to the kitchen. "We're knocking it down."

Will scratched his head. "What for, son? Looks fine to me."

"It'll open up the place more. That one, too." Kyle pointed to the opposite wall and unrolled a set of blueprints on the makeshift plywood table he'd set up. He pointed to the little box marked "dining room". "This wall is load bearing. We'll have to support it while we're waiting for the beam to be delivered from the lumber yard. The other one is okay, so it shouldn't be a problem."

Will stared at him, perplexed. "You sure you want to do this? You were so adamant about having a separate room for your pool table. You must have argued with the architect a dozen times about it."

Kyle chuckled. "I'll build a game room in the basement. This is going to be a dining room."

He dipped the brush into the can of Polyurethane on the floor and tapped the ends against the can, draining the bristles of excess liquid. With care, he ran the brush along the fine oak trim he'd already stained a rich golden-honey color.

Knocking down the walls had been a good move. He hadn't been aware that the downstairs rooms felt closed in before he'd made the change. A pool table off the kitchen and family room had been of bigger interest when he'd made the design change to the house. Someplace for the guys to escape but still remain close to the essentials of life, namely a well-stocked refrigerator.

More than once during the week, he'd second-guessed himself for changing his house to suit Lauren's design. After all, she wouldn't be the one to live here, so why should he care if a poolroom off the kitchen didn't make sense? It made perfect sense to him. But now, seeing how the results of the last few days' work transformed the rooms, he knew that Lauren had been one hundred percent correct in suggesting the change.

"Maybe all that's needed is a woman's touch," he said to himself, answering his own musings. And not just any woman. One special woman.

Kyle glanced over at Max, who was lavishing great attention on a rawhide bone. "She doesn't want to get involved, boy."

Given what she'd told him about Kristen's father, he realized he was no different in his youth. Would he have done the right thing back then? If he was at all honest with himself, he'd have to say no. He groaned at the realization of that. And if Lauren believed that Kristen's father could never change, then after hearing about all his past indiscretions, maybe she believed that of him as well. Most of his skeletons had already danced their way out of the closet, thanks to his parents. He couldn't blame her for being gun-shy.

He eyed the empty rooms, mesmerized by the light spilling into every corner. He then let his gaze drift out the window to the back yard. The smooth snow from a few days ago was now crumpled from Max trampling through, trying to chase squirrels. He noticed a set of new deer tracks cut in the snow leading to the back porch where he'd placed apples a few days ago. He could just picture one of those wooden swing sets with a tower and bright-colored canvas roof he'd seen at the lumber yard out there with Kristen, Julie, and Scotty playing. Maybe even a few little ones of his own running around or playing in a sandbox.

And Lauren. She'd make her mark all over this house. He could just see her arranging roses in a vase at the table. She'd like roses. She seemed like the kind of woman who'd place a fragrant rose or two on his pillow just before climbing into bed. Maybe he'd make a rose bed out back so she could pick fresh roses...

Wait a minute, Preston! You share some hot chocolate with the woman, sing a song or two, and already you've got her moving in! Hell, he'd already given up his pool room and all she did was come for dinner. "She doesn't want to get involved." He muttered the words over and over again like a mantra but it wouldn't sink in.

He knew what he wanted. A family. And he was pretty sure he wanted Lauren to be part of it. Before he took another plunge, he had to find out if Lauren wanted it, too.

Lauren reached the second floor landing, hoisting a laundry basket filled with clean clothes just as she heard the phone ring in her apartment.

"Krissy, could you run for the phone, hon?" She'd have to ditch the clothes if she had any chance of catching whoever was calling. "I left the door open."

Kristen moved her little legs and ran up the stairs ahead of Lauren.

Lauren couldn't help but wonder who would be calling her and suddenly felt angry with herself for hoping. Her Christmas cards had gone out in the mail on Tuesday, four days ago. She'd picked out a special card for her parents and made sure to include one of Kristen's school pictures this year. It was Saturday. They must have gotten the card by now. *Maybe this year they'll call.* She steeled herself for disappointment as she scaled the remaining treads.

Drawing in a deep breath of air, she dropped the laundry basket. "Who was on the phone, honey?" she asked as she emptied her lungs.

Kristen swung the phone in her hand. "No one."

"They hung up?"

"I said 'hello' and I heard 'click'." Kristen blinked her eyes and squeezed her fingers as she demonstrated.

Lauren propped herself against the doorjamb. "It was probably a wrong number," she muttered with a sigh.

Why did she keep doing this to herself? It had been almost seven years. She never talked to her parents unless she called and even then it was always so awkward. Why should this year be any different?

"They'll call back, right, Mommy?" Kristen dropped the phone in its cradle and bounced on the sofa.

"No jumping, Krissy! You know the rules," she snapped.

Kristen stopped bouncing and stared at Lauren and she immediately regretted her harsh words. It wasn't Kristen's fault she'd made a mess of her relationship with her parents.

She felt like a heel, yelling at Kristen the way she did. Was it just her own guilt or did every parent feel this way? Just once, she'd love to be able to sit down with her mother and confide in her, talk the way they used to do before she'd made her life such a mess.

"Sorry, honey." Lauren shut the door before sitting down on the sofa. Kristen climbed into her lap and wrapped her arms around her neck. "What do you say we skip the laundry and play Barbies for a while?"

Kristen's eyes flew open. "Yeah!"

Lauren heard a knock on the door just as she finished making some peanut butter and jelly sandwiches for lunch. She licked the grape jelly smeared on her fingers as she shuffled her way to the door. "Coming!" she called out when the knock sounded again.

She swung the door open, still sucking on her index finger. The cold air coming up from the hall blew into her face before she met Kyle's ice blue gaze.

He glanced behind her to Kristen, who was sitting on the floor with her dolls, then back to Lauren again. One corner of his mouth turned up as he whispered, in a voice much too sexy for Lauren, "Mind if I do that sometime?"

She quickly pulled her finger out of her mouth. Damn. All he had to do was show up and he had her second guessing herself. She stepped back with wild thoughts of Kyle's mouth on her fingers...and more. "What do I owe this visit to?" Fluttering her moist fingers by her side, she tried her best to act as nonchalant as her reeling body would allow.

"I missed you. Did you miss me?" He smiled and cocked his head to one side, a lock of blond hair falling over his forehead.

She wished he wouldn't do that.

Instead of answering him, she shot him a sardonic look. Apparently everything she'd said last weekend had fallen on deaf ears.

He shrugged. "I called, but no one answered."

A pain stabbed at her heart. It wasn't her parents who'd phoned after all. Pointing to the unfolded clothes in the laundry basket still sitting by the sofa, she said, "I was doing the laundry."

He gave a quick nod. "I thought Kristen might like to go sledding with the kids this afternoon."

Kristen, who'd been totally engrossed in picking out a new outfit for her latest Barbie doll, shot her head up with the mention of her name. Within a matter of seconds, she was on her feet, tugging on Lauren's sleeve and begging, "Pleeeeeeaze."

Lauren let out a sigh in defeat and knotted her arms across her chest. "She hasn't eaten lunch yet."

"That's okay. Mom made a picnic lunch for the kids," Kyle said.

"Yeah, Mommy, can I go play with Julie?"

Lauren looked down at Kristen's puppy dog eyes and rumpled her blond curls. "I thought we would get a Christmas tree today, hon."

Kristen's expression drooped, along with it, Lauren's heart. There was no way Kristen would enjoy finding the perfect Christmas tree if she was thinking about the fun she was missing with her friend.

Staring back at Kyle, she jutted out her chin. "How are you going to have a picnic? It's ten degrees outside," she argued.

"It's at least twenty-five and they're having the picnic inside my house. They'll be sledding out back." He smiled at Kristen and then at Lauren. Damn, he knew she wasn't going to win this one, she fumed inwardly. And he was enjoying it!

Puffing her cheeks, she threw her hands up in resignation. "Go get your snow pants on, Krissy."

It didn't take more than a heartbeat for Kristen to scoot to her room. Within seconds, Lauren heard the sound of drawers opening and closing. No doubt half Kristen's wardrobe would be piled high on her bed before she was done dressing.

She met Kyle's gaze head on. "You play dirty."

He laughed and said in a low voice, "I play to win."

Does that include me? No, she didn't want to know the

answer to that one.

She glanced down at her navy sweatpants and sweat shirt. “If we’re going sledding, I guess I should change, too.”

“That’s a good idea, but we’re not going sledding,” he informed her. “Just the kids. My parents are downstairs in the van. They’ll be taking them out.”

“Oh. I thought we’d be going with them.” The thought of being alone in the apartment felt strange to Lauren. She couldn’t remember ever being here without Kristen and she wasn’t sure she’d welcome the feeling.

“I was hoping we could spend some time alone.”

Of course. Deaf ears. Were all men this way? Or just the ones that she had an incredible magnet to attract? “I don’t think that’s a good idea,” she said.

“Didn’t you say you still had a lot of shopping to do for Christmas?”

“Yes, but-”

“It would be the perfect time to get it done. You’ve got a free baby-sitter for the day. And Kristen is going to have a great time with-”

“Okay, okay. I hear you.” She held up her hand as a sign of truce.

His eyes smiled his pleasure. “Anyway, I’d hardly call shopping a date.”

Despite her protest and words to the contrary to him last weekend, she did welcome the idea of being with Kyle. Only problem was, it also scared her to death. He’d come dangerously close to kissing her last weekend. Part of her was beginning to wish he had and that was not a good sign. She didn’t know if she had the strength to ward off another advance.

“Give me a minute to change.”

An hour later, they walked along Main Street in Sturbridge, perusing the displays in the specialty shop windows.

Kyle pointed to a small Cape Cod-style house tucked behind some craft stores along the main road. “I bought that house ten years ago. That’s the one that started it all for me,” he said. “I was still at UMass then."

"Business major, right?"

"Yep. How'd you know?"

"Lucky guess. How did you do it?"

He laughed. "I almost flunked."

"No, I mean buying the house."

"Luck really," he said modestly. "I read about the property in the paper. It was owned by the bank and in need of repair. I pitched the idea to my father over dinner one night and he thought it showed promise. He backed me on the venture with the bank." He shook his head. "I still can't believe he did it, but he did."

Lauren smiled. "He believed in you."

"Yeah, well, I had given him plenty of reason not to, but it all worked out in the end. I couldn't have done it without him." Kyle pointed to a large post and beam building on the other side of the road. "There is a great antique toy shop next to the Outlets."

He took her hand and guided her across the street toward the newer Outlet shops. All the buildings shared a style that mirrored the old time charm that made the area famous.

Lauren couldn't help but wonder how her life would have turned out if her father had given her the same kind of support. Maybe she would have gone to college and become the architect she'd dreamed of becoming.

A gust of wind whipped in her face, chilling her to the bone. As they walked along the brick path, Lauren realized that the little house Kyle spoke of wasn't the little Cape Cod-style home she'd thought it was when he first pointed it out. The front porch boasted a bright red sign announcing a 25% off sale of hand crafted furniture.

"You bought a furniture store?" Lauren asked.

"No, it was a residential home at the time. None of these newer buildings were here when I bought it. The carpenter I sold this building to had been working out of his basement for years, selling his pieces at the Brimfield Outdoor Antique Show. Have you ever been?" he asked.

"Yes, we went last fall. I've never seen so many antiques in my life," Lauren said, remembering the acres upon acres of outdoor booths where antiques and collectibles of every kind were bartered tri-annually.

Pointing to the furniture store, he commented, "We built a workshop out back for him before the sale and now he works and sells his furniture right here. It needed some work, but being right across the street from Old Sturbridge Village, I knew it would be worth the risk. A year later, they broke ground for the newer stores. That's when I sold it for twice what I paid. The profit helped me buy the next property and things just snowballed from there on in."

In the distance, Lauren heard the faint sound of voices singing *Jingle Bells.* The voices grew louder as they walked, until she saw a small crowd of people walking up the brick lane.

An announcement came over the loudspeaker that the Sturbridge High School Choir was performing the finale of its Christmas pageant in the courtyard.

"I thought I heard music." Kyle tugged her by the arm and laughed. "You're on."

Lauren gasped. "What are you talking about?"

"Come on. You sang so good last week at the tree lighting ceremony, I'm sure they wouldn't mind one more person."

She ground her feet in, but he was too strong and practically dragged her along. "Kyle Preston, don't you dare!"

He gave a hardy laugh. *He was enjoying this!*

Kyle stopped a student passing out lyric sheets and handed it to Lauren.

"I have no intention of singing, Kyle."

"Then I'll sing."

"Now I'm really going to be embarrassed," she teased as she laughed nervously.

In the courtyard was a stage decorated with evergreen garland and gold bows. In front of the stage were several rows of folding chairs arranged in rows. They stood in the back as most of the seats were already taken.

"For our final number," the conductor said, addressing the crowd, "we'd like to solicit your help. Please join in with the words, if you know them, or hum the tune. It's a song I'm sure you're all familiar with." Turning back to the choir, he lifted his baton and the song began.

The crowd sang along to *Deck the Halls*. After the first round of fa-la-la-la-la's the choir stepped down from the stage and began walking along the brick lane, two by two. A small group of people from the crowd joined behind the choir as they passed.

Kyle gripped Lauren's hand. "Come on."

"No, I can't," Lauren said, giggling. Something about the day, the moment, seemed enchanting. Being with Kyle, she felt light as a winged dove soaring to the clouds.

"Why not?"

The afternoon sun danced in his eyes and her breath caught in her throat. "Because you're crazy."

He gave her a lopsided grin. "Just crazy for you." He squeezed her hand.

An elderly couple who'd been seated in front of them gestured for them to join in. "Tis the season," the gentleman sang, then said, "Come on."

They moved shoulder to shoulder down the brick lane with the crowd of carolers, singing and laughing as they went. Lauren couldn't help but steal a quick glance at Kyle as they walked in formation. His face radiated a smile so bright, it was as though he were intoxicated by the moment. A feeling Lauren couldn't deny had consumed her as well.

Their eyes met and held for a lingering moment and his expression changed. What she saw was the etchings of raw human emotion nakedly revealed on the lines of Kyle's face. It should have frightened her, but to her surprise it only added to the mounting desire welling up inside her.

What she saw did not frighten her. What she wanted in return did.

~6~

A smoldering fire burned in the depths of Kyle's ice blue eyes and suddenly, Lauren wondered just what it would be like to be engulfed by that flame. Hearing her heart beat like a timpani in her ear, she sucked in a breath and held it, before emitting a cloud of mist.

Deck the hall...

His lips didn't move. He was no longer paying attention to the music coming over the loudspeaker or the people singing. He focused on her and her alone. She wasn't sure when it happened, but they stopped moving and the carolers drifted pass them down the lane. She forced a chilled breath deep into her lungs and trembled with anticipation.

He bent his head and his mouth came over hers like a gentle summer breeze caressing her skin. Hot, moist and oh, so inviting. Kyle placed his hand on the nape of her neck and deepened the kiss, seeking what she never thought she had to give. His scent filled her head and sent her senses reeling. He was warm and hard against her softness and she heard herself moan with delight. Or was that him? She didn't know...and didn't care. All she knew was that she'd been swallowed by an all consuming passion that now threatened to dissolve her. And she didn't care if it did.

She heard his sharp intake of breath amid the music blaring over the speakers as he pulled away. His breathing was ragged, as was her own, she realized. With his hand still at the back of her head, he gently caressed her neck and combed his fingers through her hair before dropping his hand.

He held her gaze and she wondered what he saw written in her expression. A gust of wind lifted her hair and broke the trance between them.

"We'd better get going." She turned away and looked into the faces of people who were filing away from the courtyard. For a moment she'd forgotten where and who she was or the presence of people around her. Suddenly, she felt as if she was an item on display, although she was sure none of the strangers were paying any real attention to them.

Shaking her hair, she tried to regain her composure. "I don't want to get back too late." She spun around and walked toward the stores.

"We have all the time in the world, Lauren," Kyle said to her back. She knew he wasn't talking about hours in the day. Within seconds, his hand was clasped around hers in a tight hold. It was clear he had no intentions of letting her take flight from him after their kiss. The thing that she couldn't figure out was why she didn't want to.

As they walked down the brick path, they passed a store window displaying an assortment of gift-wrapped packages under a silver-limbed Christmas tree. Although the red and green ornaments were festive and shimmered under the display lights, it held little charm.

"That's the saddest tree I've ever seen," Kyle said, staring at the display. "I like cranberries and popcorn, myself."

She looked up at him in awe that he was thinking the same thoughts as her own. "And gingerbread cookies with gold ribbon," she added.

He smiled. "Scotty made a star out of aluminum foil in preschool a few years back. You should see his face when Mom puts it on the tree."

"Hey, that's a good idea. We don't have a tree topper. I'll have to remember that when we put up our tree. Oh, look!" Lauren dropped Kyle's hand and raced to the toy store display window a few yards away.

Behind the glass was a magical winter wonderland. A pair of moving Santa and Mrs. Claus figurines stood in the center of the display surrounded by miniature elves buried in a sea of fake snow. A toy train, set on tracks suspended from the ceiling, disappeared into a tunnel before coming back to the display for the outdoor viewing.

But the thing that caught Lauren's attention was the magnificent antique doll house. It was every little girl's dream come true, from the Farmers porch with swing, to the miniature furniture and people all set up inside. The house opened on hinges, giving ample space for a child of any age to sit and rearrange the pieces. She could just envision her and Kristen sitting on the floor of her bedroom, playing with it for hours.

"Krissy would just love that." Lauren kept her eyes on the doll house and felt Kyle's hand on her shoulder, giving it a gentle squeeze.

"I've got the feeling you would, too," he said softly. "Let's go inside and take a look." Kyle led her to the double doors, opened one, and waited for her to proceed inside.

Pulling the scarf from her neck, Lauren groaned and trudged to the display. There was no sense falling in love with this doll house, she thought with a sigh. Without even looking at the price tag, she knew that it was far beyond her reach.

"Beautiful detail," Kyle said in admiration as he bent down and pulled the white tag, holding it out for her to inspect the price.

Lauren's shoulders sagged when she read the numbers. Just as she expected, it was well beyond her financial reach. She would never be able to afford spending an entire month's rent no matter how perfect a gift it would make.

As if reading her mind, Kyle offered, "What do you say I pick it up as a gift for Kristen?"

She glared at him, more angry with herself for not having the means to enjoy giving such a luxury than at his attempt at charity. Piqued, she knotted her scarf around her neck. "We've already been through this, Kyle. I won't take your money."

She spun on her heels and pushed through the store door with force tantamount to her anger. When she reached the sidewalk, he caught her arm and twisted her around to meet his gaze head on.

"Hey, this is no big deal. Why won't you let me do something for you?" he huffed. His drawn expression told her he was hurt by her rejection, not angry.

Seeing his reaction defused some of her anger, but did nothing to squash her pride. "It is to me. I should be able to give my child what she needs without any help from you or anyone else."

Damn, but she's stubborn, Kyle fumed inwardly. If it wasn't for the fact that he knew her pride would be destroyed, he'd run right back into the store and buy the doll house despite her protest. But he knew she'd hate him for it. And he couldn't bear that.

His mind raced. If she won't take the money from him, maybe he could convince her to take a store credit. "Wait a minute. Let's go back in and see if we can work something out with the manager."

"What good with that do? I still can't afford it."

She sighed and his heart broke in two. It was such a simple thing, buying this damned doll house, yet she acted like she'd be giving up her first born child by accepting his gift. It was so ironic, he thought. Lauren was so unlike any of the women he'd known who were always too eager for him to pull out his checkbook for them.

"Maybe not in one lump sum, but spread out over time, you-"

"I can't, Kyle." He sensed her embarrassment as her gaze dipped to the ground and she shoved her hands deep into her coat pocket. "The store is not going to give me credit on my salary. It's no use even trying. Even if they did, I doubt I'd be able to make the payments."

Kyle looked back at the doll house in the window. There had to be a way without Lauren feeling that she was compromising her ideals.

Suddenly, this doll house held all the magic of Christmas. It wasn't just a toy, it was a symbol, a home. He envisioned his house and the fantasy he'd created earlier of Lauren and Kristen living there with him. As he peered back at her, he saw a sheen of moisture in her eyes. "Then I'll give you credit," he said, determination spurring him on.

She sucked in a deep breath, her jaw set, and started to protest, but he put up his hand and cut her off at the pass. There was no way he was going to lose this battle.

"Hear me out, lady, this is not charity. This is a loan." He sucked in a frosty breath and waited for her next move.

She tilted an eyebrow and he thought he saw a spark of hope settling in her eyes. Good. It was just what he needed to bring the deal home.

"It will be strictly business. A little like some of the wheeling and dealing I use to buy property. It's called creative financing."

"Oh, I see." She rolled her eyes. "And what kind of creative financing are you going to give me? Nonexistent payment plan? No thank you."

The skepticism in her tone did nothing to deplete his resolve. He found the energy and spunk that made him what he was today come back to him tenfold with her stubbornness. She was a challenge, indeed, but no tougher than any of the other challenges he'd faced in his life.

"We can figure out a workable payment plan. Whatever you decide you can afford comfortably." He could almost hear the wheels in her head spinning, contemplating, then deciding.

"With interest, right? I won't take-"

"I know, I know, you won't take charity." He puffed his cheeks. "No interest."

She raised her eyebrows and stuck out her chin.

"Instead of interest," he bargained, placing his index finger to his cheek, "you spend the holidays with me and my family." There. He'd just used his trump card. How could she pass up a family Christmas?

Her face softened, the wildcat fire in her ebbed away and was replaced by pain. "Christmas is a time for family."

"And friends. There'll be lots of people at my parents' Christmas Eve. You and Kristen can stay in the spare room at their house."

"You can't just invite me into your parents' home, you know," Lauren argued.

Does this woman back down to anything?

"They already invited you for Christmas Eve. I told them you'd be coming for Christmas, too." It was a lie, he hadn't told them any such thing. But he had her on the run and he wasn't about to let her slip through his fingers now by telling her so. Besides, he knew his parents wouldn't mind her staying the night. The more the merrier as the saying goes.

The tension in her face eased and she gazed up at him, searching his expression. "Why do you keep doing this?"

Because I can't think of anything I want more than being with you on Christmas morning, Lauren Alexander. He thought about saying the words, but in doing so, he knew she'd just make up some excuse for not spending the holidays with him. The thought of her and Kristen being alone was something he couldn't bear. The thought of him being without them suddenly seemed just as bad.

Her wide eyes glistened and a smile tugged at the corner of her lips. "What if I'd said no?"

"Does that mean you're saying yes?"

She poked him in the ribs and chuckled. "You first."

He hesitated for a second, weighing his words. He leaned into her and said softly, "I would have been incredibly disappointed."

Her eyes flew open with surprise. After the kiss they just shared, how could she not know how he'd feel?

"Really?" she whispered.

He shrugged. "Yes." Why did he suddenly feel like he was standing buck naked on the street corner bearing his soul? Maybe because, in a way, he just did. He was surprised at how good it felt.

She glanced back at the doll house in the window, a twinkle of glee sparkling in her eyes. "It's a deal." Lauren extended her hand to his and, with a nod of her head, gave it one hard shake to cement their deal.

With their hands still clasped together, they pushed through the toy store doors to buy the antique doll house. This simple toy was much more than just a child's plaything. It was a symbol, the beginning of an upward climb toward trust. And he had every intention of reaching the top.

During the ride back to his house, Kyle couldn't help but revel in the triumph that lingered in him. The sun was still bright in the sky, glistening on the snow with a blinding sheen. He made the turn onto Tower Hill Road and stole a glance at Lauren as she looked out the window. He couldn't believe the transformation that had come over her this afternoon.

Despite what she'd said about not wanting to get involved, she did have feelings for him. What transpired between them when they'd kissed was not something that could be imagined. It was raw volcanic emotion. Damn, but this woman could spark a fire below his belly that would blow a mountain top sky high. And he was sure it was something they both had experienced.

She looked out the window at the scenery as they drove, a hint of a smile still dancing in her eyes. Several times he'd caught her turning to look at the box they'd carefully covered with a blanket and tucked in the back of the Jeep so Kristen wouldn't suspect anything. He couldn't keep from smiling himself. Not because it was the perfect gift for Kristen, but because of the milestone they'd achieved between the two of them in purchasing it.

Lauren was beginning to trust him, if only in a small way. This one baby step they'd taken felt like a giant leap. If he had his way-and he was determined he would-this was just the first of many leaps forward.

The street was lined with hundred-year-old maple trees displaying sturdy branches, now bare of the leaves that colored them each autumn. Just beyond a large farm was his property. He'd always loved this road. He hoped Lauren would, too. Blood raced through his veins in anticipation. He'd work the last two years designing, then constructing the home he planned to live in alone. Why should he care if she liked the house?

But he did care. He wanted her to like what he'd done because he hoped that someday she and Kristen would be living there with him.

"This is it." Kyle pointed to the custom two story home set back from the road.

Lauren leaned forward in her seat and sighed. Kyle's home was exactly how she'd imagined it. Completely breathtaking. She recalled her first reaction when looking at the blueprints in his apartment and how he'd described the yard. The driveway started at the far end of the property and meandered back a few hundred feet to a three car garage. Clusters of white birch trees were scattered in the front yard as if they'd been purposely landscaped that way. Lauren closed her eyes and could just imagine the vivid colors of tiger lilies and garden phlox glowing against the white tree bark in summertime. It was an awesome effect. Opening her eyes again, she saw the blanket of white covering the ground, no doubt hiding any blemishes to the earth caused by the ongoing construction.

From the outside, the house looked completed, but Kyle had mentioned it needing the finishing touches.

"It's beautiful, Kyle." She felt breathless and was sure she sounded that way as well.

Kyle smiled his pleasure as he parked his Jeep behind the van. "What's first, the grand tour or a ride down the hill on a Flexible Flyer?"

"Call me a wimp, but I'll take the tour."

After an impressive review of the house, Kyle joined his father in the back yard to help the children apply the finishing touches to a snowman they'd been working on. Lauren and Judy stayed in the kitchen sipping the last of the hot chocolate from the thermos.

"I don't know how you do it," Lauren said. "I'm always exhausted by the end of the day and I only have one child, you have four!"

Judy laughed. "Some days it might as well be ten."

"How do you do it?"

"I really felt the work when Julie and Scotty were born. I'm sure Kyle has told you all my children are adopted."

Lauren nodded.

"The little ones were the only two that Will and I have raised since birth. The list for adopting a newborn in Massachusetts is long, so we had quite a wait. Zoey was four when she came to live with us. We adopted her a year later." Judy patted Lauren on the shoulder. "Brace yourself for the teenage years. You'll need all your strength and patience then, my dear."

Lauren groaned inwardly. No one had to tell her how trying a teenager could be. All she had to do was remember her own adolescence.

"I'm glad you came into my son's life." Judy propped herself against the island counter in the center of the kitchen and eyed Lauren. She'd seen the same look before, at dinner last weekend, but dismissed it as simple kindness. Now she recognized it as a warm affection towards her.

She couldn't help but chuckle. "Kyle's a pretty tenacious guy."

"That's my son for you. I admire that in him. It's helped him along in life. Although Zoey may not see that as the most admirable trait in her big brother." Judy began tossing the leftover paper plates from their afternoon picnic into a trash bag. "But where you're concerned, I'd have to say I approve."

Heat crept from her toes to her cheeks as she remembered how Kyle had kissed her earlier. "We're, ah, just friends."

Judy stopped in mid-motion and stared at Lauren. "Hmm. Well, whatever it is, I think you're good for him."

She turned away from Judy's scrutiny and stared out the window, fixing her gaze on the snowman project. "He likes to help people. I don't think I had anything to do with that."

Judy chuckled. "Ask Zoey and she'll tell you he likes to help a little too much, to the point of being downright meddlesome."

Lauren felt a grin tug at her lips. She'd actually thought the same thing herself over the past week.

"Unfortunately, people can easily take advantage of a generous heart."

Lauren snapped her gaze at Judy.

"No, no. I don't mean you, Lauren," Judy said quickly.

"You mean the woman he built this house for?"

It was Judy's turn to be surprised. "Debra was a nice girl. A little needy, though. She wanted much more than even Kyle could give."

Curiosity won over Lauren's pride. "Look at this house. How much more could she possibly have wanted?"

Judy leaned her hip against the counter. "All of him." She sighed. "Debra came from a large family. She was one of eight and they didn't have much. Attention was at a premium, I suspect. She liked Kyle's generosity as long as it was focused on her. With her family being so large, Kyle had assumed family was important to her."

"But it wasn't?"

Judy shook her head. "She didn't want family around and Kyle can't live without it. Family is very important to him. He likes being in the middle of everything, doing things for people."

That much was evident to Lauren. Since the moment she met Kyle Preston, he was doing things for her.

When she said nothing, Judy went on. "Kyle's heart is in the right place. I make no bones about the fact that I'm proud of what he's accomplished given his troubled childhood."

"He mentioned he came to live with you when he was twelve," Lauren offered. Part of her hoped to gain some insight into Kyle's past. Although he'd always spoken fondly of his adoptive parents, he had yet to speak of his life before he came to live with them. She was disappointed when Judy did not elaborate any further.

"Trusting didn't come easy for Kyle. At first, he did everything in his power to push us away. I know he was afraid of getting hurt again." Judy sighed as she bent down to pick up the blanket on the floor. Lauren followed and helped with the folding. "Then he did everything he could to win our approval, as if that would make us love him. He could never quite believe he already had our love."

Lauren knew those feelings well. Except she knew she didn't have her parents' approval. Their brand of tough love sent her out on the streets when she needed them the most. Despite the pain it caused, she'd give anything to get past the tension dividing them and have them back in her life again.

After dropping the blanket into the picnic basket and adding the empty thermos, Judy continued. "This is a beautiful house, but I don't think he was ready to make such a move. He did it to please

Debra." Judy shrugged. "That's just the way he is."

Lauren felt a prick at her heart with Judy's words. After the afternoon they'd spent together, she let herself believe that maybe, just maybe she'd be able to allow herself to get close to Kyle. The kiss they'd shared just about rocked her world with its intensity. And she'd be lying to herself if she said she didn't want more. Earlier, as she walked through the house that he built, she foolishly let her mind daydream about what it would be like if she and Kristen lived here as Kyle's family.

Well, now is the time for the old kick-in-the-butt reality check, girl. If what Judy said was true, and there was no reason for Lauren to believe otherwise, then Kyle was just being himself, doing what he always did. He was just trying to please her.

Judy hooked the picnic basket in her arm and walked into the dining area, inspecting the open design. The pungent fumes of Polyurethane and stain hung heavy in the air. "So this is what he's been working on so diligently this week." She waved her arm around the room.

Lauren had noticed the rooms were open, void of the walls that she'd seen in the original design. She didn't say anything about her suggestion to make the change. Like he'd done for Debra, had Kyle made this change just to please her? "I like how it makes the rooms feel," she said instead.

Judy gazed at her and smiled warmly. "I like it, too."

~7~

"I want the most beautiful one you have," Kyle said to the man mummified in a cold weather parka. He could barely see his face beneath the furry hood. "Just point me in the direction and I'll cut it down myself."

"I've still got a couple of thirteen foot Douglas firs in the back of the farm, right near the one you cut down last week." The salesman, who Kyle had known for years, was the owner of the tree farm.

"No, not that big. A seven foot tree, nice and full all around would be great." He rubbed his gloved hands together in an attempt to ward off the cold. It had been snowing off and on for the past two days. The trek up to the back of the farm would be too difficult with all the snow.

"We've got a whole farm of seven footers. Pretty ones, too. Just take your pick."

With saw in hand, Kyle plowed a fresh path through the snow in search of the perfect Christmas tree. Forty-five minutes later, he'd cut and purchased what he thought was just that.

He just hoped Lauren would be home, he thought as he drove over to her place to delivered it. He had attempted to call Lauren several times, but hadn't been able to reach her. Earlier in the week, he hadn't thought much about it when the answering machine picked up and he heard her prerecorded voice suggesting he leave a message. By Thursday evening, he began to get the distinct feeling that maybe she was avoiding him.

Okay, so maybe he'd laid things on a little thick by commandeering her into dinner, hijacking her to go shopping, kissing her... He'd lay it on as thick as he could if he could kiss her sweet lips again.

Most men would bring flowers to court a lady, he thought as he removed the rope securing the freshly cut Christmas tree to the top of his Jeep. He'd save the roses for another time. Hell, he'd build her a whole rose bed out back so she could have fresh roses everyday.

Today they were going to decorate a Christmas tree. He gripped the trunk in the center of the tree and pulled until the tree was on the sidewalk in front of Lauren's home.

As he dragged the tree beside him, he saw her car parked in the driveway. Good, no answering machines, no excuses. *She's home.*

Familiar with the sticky door, he clutched the handle and yanked hard. "That gets fixed once and for all," he muttered as he struggled with the branches. Once he managed to pull the tree through the doorway, he dragged it up the three flights of stairs to Lauren's attic apartment.

Lauren pulled the afghan snug to her chest and shivered. She groaned. This was the worst time in the world to be getting sick. She'd worked a week full of overtime just so she could take some time off after Christmas to spend with Kristen. She shivered again and sneezed.

Kristen pulled a tissue from the box and handed it to Lauren. "God bless you, Mommy."

"Thank you, sweetie," she said just as she heard a knock at her door. She twisted her legs off the sofa and padded across the floor.

As she swung the door open, the cold breeze coming up from

the hallway caused her to shiver. She closed her eyes and sneezed. Opening her eyes again, she frowned.

"Is there a person behind this tree?" she asked.

"Yes, ma'am." Kyle's gloved hand weeded its way through the branches, pulling them down so Lauren could see his face.

"Kyle, what have you done?!"

"I brought you a Christmas tree."

"I can see that. But..."

He tried forcing the tree through the door with visible difficulty. The branches were just too wide. "But what? Did you already get one?" he asked, grunting.

"No."

"Great. When I couldn't reach you this week I thought maybe you were out getting one."

She sniffed, yanked a tissue from the box on the bookcase, and blew her nose. "I had to work late every day. I'm taking Christmas week off so that I can spend some time with Krissy."

Still struggling in the doorway, he said, "Good idea. Do you have a tree stand?"

She felt her lips lift to a smile. She sucked in her cheeks to keep him from seeing her amusement with the situation. "Yes, but there is no way that tree is going to fit in here."

"Sure it will," he said confidently. With exuberance he squeezed the tree through until he was in the living room. "When I was out at the farm, I could just envision this tree all lit up in the corner of the room. It's going to fit just perfect next to the..."

With her hand to her face, Lauren bit her lip and chuckled. Kyle thoughtfully inspected the corner on the other side of the bookcase and frowned.

"It's not going to fit," he muttered and propped the tree against the closed door.

"Exactly."

"It looked great in my head."

Kristen bounced over to Lauren's side and waved to Kyle. "Is it ours, Kyle?"

He crouched down to her level and rumpled her downy curls.

"Sure is, scooter." He lowered his voice. "But it looks like we're going to have to perform some heavy duty surgery before it'll fit."

Kristen giggled.

Lauren sniffed and rubbed her watering eyes. "We planned on going out tomorrow."

"Doesn't look like you'll be going anywhere with that cold. How long have you been like this?" he asked, a hint of concern coloring his tone.

"It started yesterday. I think this is the worst of it. It'll pass." She waved her hand to make light of it, but Kyle just grimaced.

"I'm sure it will when you get some rest."

"I don't have time to rest. Look at this place." With a sweep of her hand gesturing to the room, she said, "Just a few days before Christmas and I haven't decorated the apartment."

"There is plenty of time for that tomorrow when you're feeling better. Right now, you're going to rest." He gripped her shoulders and twisted her around before leading her to the sofa. If she'd been feeling herself, she would've balked at his command. But given her current state, she had to admit she welcomed someone else taking charge. "Kristen and I will keep busy while you get some sleep."

"You don't need to take care of Kristen," she protested.

"You're the one who needs to be taken care of." He held up his hand when she began to protest. "What good is taking time off to be with your daughter if you get pneumonia, which is exactly what you'll have if you run yourself into the ground."

"But-"

"I'm not taking no for an answer, so don't waste your breath. You need all you can get." He handed her the box of tissues and picked up the afghan, carefully placing it over her shivering body. It should have made her feel better, but it did nothing to dispel the chills causing her to shake.

"What will you do?" she asked. She plopped down on the sofa, plumping the throw pillow before laying her head down.

"We'll get out of the house for a while and leave you to sleep. Maybe we'll go shopping for things to decorate the tree. Or maybe stop by my parents' so the kids can play." He gave her a lopsided grin. "Don't worry. She's going to be just fine."

Don't worry he says! That's pretty darn hard to do when for the past seven years her whole world revolved around this child.

Ten minutes later, after Kristen was bundled up warm, Kyle shut the door behind them. It was the oddest feeling she had ever known. There had always been noise and commotion of some kind in the apartment. But now, there was silence.

For the first time in years, Lauren was truly alone.

It was some time later, when she felt a cold hand against her cheek, that she realized she'd actually fallen asleep. Her eyes still heavy, she struggled to pull herself from slumber. When she lifted her lids, she was met by Kyle's worried gaze.

"You look awful." he murmured.

"Thanks a lot," she managed to say as she strained to focus on the room. Supporting the full weight of her upper body on her right arm, she looked around, ignoring the ache in her shoulders. She stopped just short of panic. "Where's Krissy?"

"Don't worry. She was having a good time with Julie." A smile tugged at his lips. "You should have heard the two of them plotting to arrange a sleep-over. I told her she could only stay if you agreed."

"We've never been separated overnight before." She pulled herself to a sitting position and groaned as her head bobbed back. Her whole body felt as if she'd been hit with a sledgehammer.

"Whoa, lady. You're burning with fever. You're not going anywhere." He coaxed her to lay down before walking away. She heard running water and cabinets opening and shutting before he was by her side again. Handing her a glass of water and two pills, he said, "Take these. They'll take your temperature down and help with the aches."

She did as she was told and handed him the empty glass with a shaky hand. Her teeth began to chatter.

"I don't know about you, but I think it's a good idea for Kristen to stay with my parents tonight."

Closing her eyes, she shook her head.

He eased himself on the sofa. "You don't want her getting sick, too."

The tenderness in his voice told Lauren he knew how hard it was for her to be separated from Kristen.

"I...think you're right."

He nodded. "She can borrow some of Julie's clothes. They're about the same size."

Her eyelids fluttered and she felt a cold compress on her forehead. "What time is it?" she asked, shivering.

"About four-thirty." He pulled up the afghan and squeezed next to her on the sofa. His body pressed against the full length of hers.

"What are you doing?" She had no strength to protest.

"You've got the chills. I'm just going to use my body temperature to warm you until you stop shaking."

Her head fell against his chest and she closed her eyes. Immediately, her body relaxed when she felt his fingers stroked her head. The heavy thump of his heartbeat set a tranquil cadence and soon rocked her to sleep.

When Kyle heard Lauren's rhythmic breathing, he eased himself off the sofa, trying his best not to disturb her. Her hair clung to the beads of sweat on her forehead. Good, he thought with relief. That was a clear sign her fever was breaking. He kissed her head before reaching for the telephone and dialing his parents' telephone number.

After two rings, Will answered, "Hello?"

"It's me," Kyle answered. "Do you mind telling Ma it's okay for Kristen to stay the night?"

Will sighed. "Sure, no problem." The slight hesitation in his father's voice was cause for alarm.

"What gives?"

After another hesitation, Will said, "Your mother had a run in with Zoey this morning. She took off with Bruce afterward. When I heard the phone, I thought maybe it was her." He heard his father's breath distort over the phone.

"Mom didn't mention anything when I was there," hc said.

"It's not like this hasn't happened before. Zoey and your mother haven't exactly seen eye to eye lately."

"Did she say when she'd be back?"

"No."

"I'll go look for her," he said, already reaching for his jacket.

"No, no. That won't be necessary. It's still early. I'm sure she's just being sixteen." He paused a moment and added. "I just don't like seeing your mother worry."

Him, too, Kyle reflected. Despite the concern for his wife, Kyle knew this thing with Zoey was making his dad crazy. He ought to know. He'd put his parents through this sort of anguish more times than he could count.

"How's Lauren feeling?" Will asked, changing the subject.

He pushed his fingers through his hair and looked over at her. Although she was asleep, she seemed restless. "Worse than this morning. She's got a nasty fever. Aches and pains."

"Your mother's soup should help."

"Yeah, I'll warm some up for her when she wakes. Hopefully it's just the twenty-four hour bug that's been going around." His mind raced ahead to his sister. "And Dad?"

"Yeah, son?"

"You will call me if you can't find Zoey, right?"

"Don't worry. She'll be home."

Kyle sat in a rocking chair and watched Lauren sleep until the shadows stretched across the room. Lifting himself up, he flicked on the lamp and paced to the kitchen area. Hearing his stomach growl, he realized he hadn't eaten since breakfast. He simmered a potful of the chicken soup his mother had given him to bring over to Lauren and sat with a bowl of it at the kitchen table. He was just finishing when he heard Lauren stir.

As she kicked the blanket off, she turned her body to face him, the blanket falling to the floor.

"That smells good," she said, her voice groggy. "That can't possible have come from my kitchen."

Kyle chuckled as he pulled another bowl from the cabinet. "Mom sent it over. You must be feeling better if you're thinking about food."

She sat up and yawned into both hands. "Much. I'm starved."

"That's a good sign."

She started to stand, then fell off balance and landed back on the couch. "Whoa."

"Better not over do it. I'll bring the soup over to you."

"Have I been asleep long?" she asked, combing her fingers through her hair as if she was suddenly self-conscious.

"A few hours." He handed her the soup bowl on a dish towel. "The bowl is hot," he warned, joining her on the sofa.

"Thanks." She took a few spoonfuls.

As Kyle gazed at her, he noticed some color had returned to her cheeks and her eyes were not as drawn. Apparently the sleep and aspirin had done their work.

She stopped eating, her gaze lingering on him for a moment. "I must look awful," she said self-consciously.

"You look beautiful," he murmured.

"Liar."

"Who me?" he teased, placing his hand over his heart in a mock gesture. He felt his smile fade. "I'd never lie to you, Lauren."

Her eyes dipped and then looked back at him. Changing the subject, she asked, "What did you and Kristen end up doing this afternoon?"

He couldn't help but smile. Kristen had wanted to get something special for Lauren, so "the girls" went shopping while he stayed back at the house with Scotty. When they returned, Kristen proudly announced that she bought some "smelly perfume" as a gift.

"I hung out at the house."

"Did you finish yet?"

He shot her a puzzled look.

"The house. It looked pretty close to being complete last weekend. There can't be much left for you to do there."

"Oh, my house. Yeah, I just need my occupancy permit and I'll be calling the movers."

"You've decided to move in after all."

He shrugged. "Maybe. But I wasn't out there today. I stayed

back at my parents'."

Silence stretched on for an uncomfortable moment.

Lauren placed the bowl on the end table and wiped her lips with the dish towel. "Remind me to thank your mom for the soup. It was great."

He nodded.

She wrapped the blanket around her shoulders and sat with her legs tucked underneath her. "Your mom mentioned your friend Chas was going to be there Christmas Eve."

He nodded.

"You two have quite a history as I understand it. Sounds like you were close."

He smiled and nodded.

"Do you see him much?"

He shot his head up to meet her probing eyes. "Not as much as I'd like. He's been living out of state for a few years. I'm glad he's moving back."

"Did something happen between you two?"

He shifted his weight as if he were uncomfortable. "Full of questions, are we?"

"Stop trying to change the subject." She tossed the dish towel at him. It bounced off his chest and landed in his lap.

"What was the subject?" he asked, giving her a mischievous grin.

"Chas. Why do get all uncomfortable when his name is mentioned?"

He shrugged. God, he hated talking about this. And by the way she was throwing questions at him, he knew that Lauren wasn't going to let it go. "I don't. Not where Chas is concerned, anyway. We had quite a reputation way back when as the bad boys of the county. I just don't like being reminded."

"The things Judy and Will talked about sounded like harmless adolescent pranks. Nothing to stop the press about. I'd hardly call you a hardened criminal."

"I stole a truck." He looked at her stone faced and saw her expression change from disbelief to shock. "Grand theft auto qualifies as a criminal felony."

She swallowed visibly.

"I didn't go to prison. Except, of course, County Jail the first night."

She fiddled with her fingers in her lap. The afghan fell from her shoulders and she quickly pulled it back. When she looked at his face again, he was relieved to see that she was not judgmental, merely nervous. "Was Chas with you?"

"Like always." He looked away and held his breath. He'd give anything if he'd been alone, but back then, he and Chas were joined at the hip. Where there was one, so was the other.

"What happened?"

"It was the night of a big town meeting. The selectmen were arguing some big issue. I don't even remember what it was." He scratched the back of his head and took a deep breath before continuing. "The Town Hall was packed. Chas and I thought it would be a great time to go night skiing at Mt. Tom. We were sure the meeting was going to go late into the night so we just *borrowed* the selectman's truck."

"Without telling him."

"Unfortunately, that was the point."

"And you got caught."

"Not when we were stealing it. We went skiing for about an hour. I was driving home, rushing to get back before the meeting was over. I was so cocky," he whispered to himself with the memory.

"You got pulled over for speeding?"

He shook his head. "I wish it were that." God, how he wished it were only that. That one incident had changed his life forever and scarred his friend. That was something he had to live with. "I hit a patch of ice and the truck spun off the road into a ditch."

Lauren gasped. "Were you hurt?"

He shook his head. "I managed to bail out before it rolled. I had some scrapes and bruises, but Chas wasn't as lucky."

"He didn't bail out?"

"He'd fallen asleep. He didn't have time to react." He

stretched his arm over the back of the sofa and nervously drummed his fingers on the upholstery. "It was quite a scene in the emergency room."

Lauren forced a smile, hoping that it would ease the tension in the room. She couldn't imagine what Kyle was feeling, the pain it had caused. But at the same time, it warmed her heart that he felt comfortable confiding in her.

"I heard Chas's parents yelling, crying...my mother crying. Do you know what that does to a person?"

Yeah, Lauren knew. Her mother had cried for a week when she told her parents she was pregnant. Images like that don't fade with time.

"Most of the night seems like a blur now, but what I remember most is my father's face. He was so angry, but his eyes were filled with disappointment." He pushed his fingers through his hair and his expression changed. "Are you still hungry?"

"Ah, no." It took her a second to comprehend that he was trying to change the subject.

"Do you want some more? There's plenty left." He leaned forward to stand, but Lauren reached out and clasped her fingers around his hand, pulling him back.

"Wait a minute."

"Would you like something to drink?"

"You're doing it again. Stop going in circles."

He sank back on the sofa and appeared aloof. "Forgive me for playing Doctor Kildare."

"Don't run away from me. Tell me what happened. This had to have happened ten, twelve years ago when you were a minor or you would have gone to prison," she said.

He gave a weak grin. "If it wasn't for my dad, I would have." The admiration he had for his father was transparent as he spoke. "I wasn't quite eighteen yet, but they could have tried me as an adult. After he bailed me out of jail, my dad took me down to the selectman's office and told him he wouldn't blame him if he pressed charges. I was a smart-ass cocky kid back then. There was no reason for him to cut me a break. Using me as an example would've been more of what I deserved."

Kyle stood up and began pacing the room. Lauren had never seen him so forlorn. Breaking open an angry wound from the past was never easy, but for someone who'd climbed his way out of that black hole like Kyle had, it was excruciating.

"My dad was humiliated, but he stood by me. Because of his reputation, not mine, the charges were dropped. I worked along side my dad for months to pay for the damage to the truck. Chas worked for months to heal."

"You paid your debt. You changed your life around for the better." She wrapped the afghan around her shoulders again. "It's a classic example of something good coming out of something bad."

He looked at her straight on and she shuddered with his intensity. "No, it's not. That's just the point."

"But you turned your life around."

"Yes, I have. It proves that people can change. Unfortunately, you can't change the past."

"I don't understand."

"I came out of that scrape the better for it. Chas didn't get that luxury."

She looked at him baffled. "But you said they dropped the charges."

"Chas almost died. He broke his neck and his right leg was crushed."

"Kyle, I'm so sorry." She didn't know what else to say.

"Believe me, so was I. I wasn't the one who was suppose to succeed in life. You know, voted most likely to be imprisoned by the senior class. How prophetic." He laughed cynically. "Chas had it all ahead of him. He lost his football scholarship after the doctors told him he'd never play. He didn't have any big dreams of going pro, but his family had three kids in college already and they couldn't exactly afford to send him once the scholarship was pulled. He never did end up going."

"You blame yourself for that, don't you?"

Regret hung heavy in the room. "I used to because it was my idea to steal the truck. Chas was angry for a long time. He had a lot to be angry about. But we got past that a long time ago."

"You didn't do it alone. Chas was right along side of you every step of the way."

He buried his fingers in his hair. "I know. But every time I see him struggling, I can't help but think he'd be a lot farther along in his life if that scholarship hadn't been pulled out from under him. When he was learning to walk again, I was out landing my first real estate deal. It's hard when you have to do it alone."

Suddenly tired again, she slumped back onto the sofa. "Don't I know it."

His expression softened. "Hey, you've done a great job with Kristen. You should feel proud of all that you've achieved on your own. I couldn't have done it."

She smiled with his compliment and leaned her head against the back of the sofa. As much as she'd been doubting herself these past few weeks, she couldn't help but feel uplifted by his admiration.

Bending toward her, Kyle felt her forehead with the back of his hand. "You're a little cooler, but you're still pale. You need to rest."

"Is that so, Dr. Kyle," she teased. "And getting me to bed is part of your prescription?"

Now that was a loaded question, Kyle thought. He could think of a hundred things he wanted do with Lauren in and out of bed that would take the edge off his wounds, but none of them would help her get any better. No matter how much he ached to act on the fantasy whirling out of control in his head and settling in a place that a woman could drive a man wild, he forced it aside. His raging libido still out of control, he swallowed hard and said, "Sleep will do you good."

Burying himself in the snowbank on the sidewalk would do him good, too, if he had any chance of actually sleeping here with Lauren in the next room.

She tossed off the afghan and he held out his hand to help her stand. She was still wearing the same gray stretch pants she'd been wearing earlier. He hadn't noticed earlier when she was under the afghan, that she'd changed out of her sweatshirt sometime during the afternoon and put on an oversized pink T-shirt. What was hard not to notice, was how little the T-shirt hid the soft curves of her breast beneath the thin cotton fabric. Her nipples, now taut and pressed against her shirt, betrayed any modesty she may have been trying to hold beneath the confines of the afghan.

Kyle squeezed her hand lightly. Touching her would lend him trouble, but he just had to feel her soft skin, connect in some way. It wasn't the time to lose himself with this woman no matter how beautiful her full lips looked in the dim lighting. Or how much he wanted to tangle his fingers in her rumpled ash hair.

"You know, you don't have to stay. This sofa isn't the world's most comfortable thing to sleep on. You'd probably have a much better night's sleep at your place." She took a deep breath and unconsciously slipped a lock of hair behind her ear.

Did she really not want him to stay? His eyes focused on her exposed earlobe and instantly wondered what it would be like to nibble on the soft flesh there, taste her skin. It made his heart race and his breathing quicken.

"I don't mind," he said. No, he didn't have to stay and torture himself with a sleepless night thinking of Lauren stretched out in a bed just mere feet from where he lay. Being as worn as she was, she'd probably sleep through the night, maybe even well into the morning. He could probably go back to his place and bring Kristen back after breakfast before she even woke up.

But he *wanted* to stay. He'd never confided in a woman before about what happened with Chas. Even Debra hadn't been really interested in how he'd changed his life around, only what he'd become. He'd always forced those dark feelings into a black hole and focused on the positive.

Tonight when Lauren forced the issue, he was ready to give it up. Surprisingly enough, it hadn't left him empty like he thought it would. It didn't change anything. But confiding in Lauren had left him strangely uplifted for the first time in years. And he knew without a doubt he'd fallen hard. He was hopelessly in love with Lauren Alexander.

He wasn't ready to break the energy between them by going home and crawling into a cold bed. Sure, he was crawling onto a cold sofa, no arms and legs to become tangled with, just wild fantasies about what may be, someday.

Soon he hoped.

But that he could handle. He'd have to.

"You may need me in the middle of the night...for something." He looked away from her for a moment, sure that his thoughts would betray his words. When he looked back, she was smiling.

"Well, since Kristen is staying at your parents' house, you may as well sleep in her bed. But I warn you," she cast a glance at the length of him, "it's a twin bed, so you may be just as cramped."

"Are you trying to get rid of me?"

"No. It's just...it's not even eight o'clock. What'll you do all night?"

A cold shower and a bucket of ice came to mind. And he was going to need them pretty damn fast if she was going to remain this close to him, staring up at him the way she did.

He waved his hand at the Christmas tree, still propped up against the wall. "There's the little matter of getting this Christmas tree set up so that it fits in the corner. That'll keep me busy for a while."

She nodded and opened her mouth to say something, but the words died on her lips and she offered up a sleepy smile instead.

He didn't push it. In her eyes, he saw the questions he knew she needed to ask and he wanted to answer. There was plenty of time for that. This was just another step forward.

~8~

The sun streamed through the blinds of Lauren's bedroom window, causing long shadow lines to stretch across the room. She forced her eyes open, feeling immediately that something was different. The full night's sleep had done her a world of good, but better health wasn't what she noticed.

The apartment was strangely quiet and it took a moment to register what was odd about this morning compared to every other day. The noise, or lack of it finally struck her with a sense of urgency. As a rule, Kristen was always the first to be up and about, which gave Lauren no real need for an alarm clock. The absence of morning cartoons filtering in from the television in the living room or the tumbling of toys from the toy box in Kristen's room gave a weird sensation to the morning.

Lauren glanced at the digital clock on the night stand next to her bed. The red numbers told her it was seven-thirty. After pushing up from the bed, she pulled a white terry robe from her closet and wrapped it snug around her body. The nightshirt she threw on last night when she went to bed was sheer gauze and fell to her upper thigh. It was not the kind of thing to go parading around in with a house guest.

Kyle. Was he even still here? She hadn't heard any signs of

stirring from him, either. Walking over the threshold into the living room, she found her suspicions were right on target. The bathroom door was wide open and the kitchen area empty. A folded blanket lay on the empty sofa. He was gone.

Swept by a sense of abandonment, she pulled the terry robe tighter and looked around the room. She tried to tell herself it wasn't a good idea for Kyle to stay last night, there was no need for him to take care of her. In the end, it had been way too easy to let him take over.

The bottom line was that, despite the need, she *wanted* him to stay. She *liked* having him around. For what reason, she didn't want to even think about.

Kyle had been busy last night while she slept, that much was evident as she scanned the apartment. In the kitchen, a bowl with nothing but a few popcorn kernels lay in the middle of the table surrounded by strings of popcorn garland. Somehow he'd managed to find her Christmas decorations in the eave and pulled out her tree stand. The Christmas tree was now *clipped* and neatly tucked in the corner, filling the space completely. Although the branches were still bare of any decoration, it held the promise of elegance and holiday cheer.

She must have slept like a rock, because she hadn't heard any commotion at all after her head hit the pillow.

After opening a cabinet and grabbing a glass, she poured herself some orange juice and leaned against the kitchen counter, drinking and listening to the quiet. Many times she longed for a morning to sleep, a quiet moment to herself. But now that she had it, she wasn't so sure she liked it at all.

She finished her juice, put the glass in the sink and stopped short, expecting to see a mountain of pots and pans and bowls from yesterday still sitting there, waiting to be cleaned. There was nothing. Kyle had done the dishes? As if needing proof, she opened cabinets and drawers to find the missing items put back in place. "Huh. Kyle did the dishes," she muttered. Although nothing was put back in exactly the right place, they were indeed washed, dried and put away. Tucked behind the gleaming chrome faucet was a folded piece of paper with her name scribbled in the middle.

She read the note.

Went to pick up Kristen and a few things from the market. Take advantage of the quiet and go back to bed. We'll be back before lunch.

She folded the note and sat down at the kitchen table. Seven-thirty and he was already up and out the door. Seven-thirty in the morning and alone, and she had no idea what to do with herself.

It was quarter to ten when Kyle and Kristen finally made it back from the market. He opened the door to Lauren's bedroom and peered in. Her eyes were closed and her hair mussed as she lay on the pillow, still sleeping soundly. Hopefully she'd have more energy when she woke up so they could decorate the tree.

He began to close the door and cringed when he heard the hinges squeak. Peering through the crack, he saw that Lauren hadn't stirred and he shut the door.

"What does this say, Kyle?" Kristen asked, straining with the weight of a five pound bag of flour in her arms.

"Do you recognize any of the letters?" he tossed back at her.

"It starts with a big F. Is it the flour?"

"Yep." He'd searched Lauren's cabinets last night and found the cupboards bare of any ingredients for making gingerbread cookies. Armed with his mother's cookie recipe and a list of ingredients and instructions, he and Kristen hit the supermarket first thing after breakfast.

Kristen pulled a bottle out of the brown paper bag. "What's this syrupy thing?"

"Molasses," Kyle told her.

"Do we need it for the cookies?"

"Yeah, but first we need a bowl."

Kristen jumped down from the kitchen chair she'd been standing on and opened the cabinet next to the stove. After a short inspection, she pulled out a small plastic bowl. "Is this going to be big enough?"

Kyle crinkled his nose. "I don't know about you but I want to eat some of these cookies, not just put them on the tree. We need a real big bowl."

Kristen look puzzled, as if she were thinking of where she could find a bowl big enough. Kyle took the bowl from her and put it back in cabinet. Crouching down to her level, he began pulling pots and pans out of the cabinet Kristen had just searched. "How about this one?" he said, holding up a large stock pot for her view.

"That's the pan Mommy uses to make spaghetti."

"Works just as good for cookies. Do you think it'll be big enough?"

Kristen smiled and nodded.

"Okay, hop on board. We're going to make some cookies."

Kyle read the ingredients out loud to Kristen as she sat on the edge of the table, her feet dangling down to the chair. "Preheat oven to 350 degrees." He looked at her over the top of his recipe card and added, "I'll do that because you're too little. Do you know where your mom keeps the mixer?"

Kristen lifted her shoulders and let them fall, before returning a blank look.

"Have you ever seen her use a mixer?"

She shook her head. "What's a mixer?"

He chuckled. "Not quite sure myself. Maybe we don't really need one. What about measuring spoons?"

Her face registered a puzzled expression.

"We'll use something from the utensil drawer. Not a problem." He positioned the bowl in front of him and read the recipe card again.

"Kyle, have you ever done this before?"

"Sure," he fibbed. "Piece a cake. We just need to dump all these ingredients into the bowl and mix them. We can do that."

He tore the seal on the flour bag and a cloud of white dust puffed in his face.

Kristen giggled. "You have white eyebrows!"

Kyle swiped the dust away with his palm and focused on the recipe card. "Two and a quarter cups of sifted flour. I wonder what you sift it through," he muttered, to himself mostly. "Half a cup of shortening. We do need measuring cups."

Kristen jumped down from the table again and pointed to a

cabinet above the sink. "There's some stuff up there."

Kyle opened the cabinet and found the measuring cups and other baking supplies he hadn't found the night before.

They made a pretty good team. He measured the ingredients and she poured them in the bowl. They both took turns stirring. Each had their share of diggings from the bowl.

Lauren sat up in bed, pulled her knees to her chest and listened to the laughter spilling in from the kitchen. The gabbing and giggling had pulled her from a deep slumber. The bass tone of Kyle's voice juxtaposed with the smooth, high pitch of Kristen's was stilling. What a wonderful sound, she thought.

"Where are the cookie cutters?" she heard Kyle ask.

"We don't use those. We use *this* cup." Kristen's response brought a smile to Lauren's lips. It had been ages since they'd made cookies, but Kristen still remembered that they always used a special plastic cup with Mickey Mouse on it as a cookie cutter. She had been guiding Kyle around the kitchen for the better part of the fifteen minutes Lauren had been awake. Lauren had no doubt which one of them was really in charge of the cookie project.

"Okay, scooter. Time for the cookie sheet," Kyle said.

Lauren heard a clunk on the linoleum floor, followed by a heavy clank on the table.

As she listened to the easy conversation between Kyle and Kristen, she felt a tear roll down her cheek. They seemed so comfortable together, just like father and daughter.

Memories of her own childhood crept into her mind. Sure her father had never baked cookies with her, he left that sort of quality time for her mother. But there were many other wonderful memories that came to mind. Memories that she had forced aside years ago, still did when it hurt too much.

Now all those memories forged to the surface as she listened to the easy interaction between Kyle and Kristen.

Kyle had a natural talent for charming women of any age. He'd succeeded in charming his way into her heart, despite her every attempt to keep him at bay. Now he was charming his way into Kristen's life.

She sighed. She wasn't so sure she liked the idea of that. If it was just her heart, well hell, she'd have nothing to lose. She could take care of herself when the inevitable happened.

And it would happen. Kyle would leave. Because men always left when things got too rough, didn't they? Loving Kyle would be the easiest, most natural thing to do. But his leaving would tear the very fabric of her heart.

Kristen was too vulnerable. Her need for a father figure, a need that Lauren had ignored, was evident in the way she interacted with Kyle. She wanted so much to have a daddy and Kyle's presence proved to be ample replacement for what her life lacked. But what would happen when he was gone? How would Kristen cope with that loss?

She threw her blankets aside and reached for the robe at the foot of her bed, slipping into it as she walked to the door. Opening the door an inch, she peered through the narrow crack at the two bakers diligently working in the kitchen.

"It's too sticky. You need more flour," she heard Kristen instruct.

Kyle tossed some flour on the table, half of which landed on the floor, the rest created a cloud of white dust. "Ooops!"

"You missed the dough." Kristen giggled. "Mommy's going to be mad."

"We'll sweep up before she's even awake. She won't ever know."

"Mommy won't know what?" Lauren opened the bedroom door and stood in the doorway, watching as the two bakers hid the contraband. Kyle twisted and hid the bowl behind his back. Kristen scurried to grab the wooden spoon and hide that behind her back. Lauren sucked in her cheeks but couldn't help but laugh. She was sure there was more flour on the two of them, and the floor, than mixed in the dough. They were positively covered.

"You're feeling better?" Kyle asked, trying to appear nonchalant.

"The sleep did some good." She perused the disaster in her

kitchen. In the short time she'd slept, Kyle and Kristen had managed to turn it upside down.

As if reading her reaction to the mess, Kyle shrugged and gave a sheepish grin. "This was sort of a surprise."

"Yeah," Kristen added, smiling as if she were quite pleased with herself for all her effort.

Lifting her eyebrows, Lauren replied, "Believe me, it is." She walked back a step and thumbed toward the bathroom. "I think I'll just take a shower if you don't mind. Let you finish up with your, ah, surprise."

After collecting a pair of her favorite blue jeans, a red turtleneck shirt and clean underwear, she withdrew to the sanctity of the bathroom. She discarded her robe and hung it on the hook on the back of the door. With her hand on the faucet, she stopped short of turning on the water. The sound of laughter coming in from the other room brought an ache to her heart.

Kyle would be such a wonderful father. He was kind and gentle and patient. And loving. Everything a child needed to feel safe and secure and loved.

Everything she needed, too, she couldn't deny.

She turned the faucet and dipped her hand under the stream of water until it was warm. When it was, she stepped into the shower and let the heat do its magic.

Thoughts of Kyle invaded her mind. If she let herself think about it, she pictured herself with a man like Kyle. Someone who'd help her bear the load, make her feel safe and secure, keep her warm at night.

But what was she doing? That wasn't going to happen. Long ago she'd conditioned herself to thinking that there wouldn't be another man in her life. Not while Kristen was young and needed so much of her time and attention.

In the short time since she'd been working at the Woodlawn Industries, she'd heard many young women talk about the men in their lives. There were some good times, some bad, but there always seemed to be the inevitable heartache that followed. She'd offered her shoulder to cry on, then listened for weeks, endlessly about how they'd never go through that again, only to have one of them come in Monday morning with news of a new man.

Sure, she'd listened to the talk and even envied a few that spoke of the true love they shared. But it always ended up the same. Like Jimmy, and like her father, the men would always leave.

And now Kyle. How was she going to feel when he walked away? She hated to admit it, but he'd opened up her heart and claimed a piece of it for himself. She cared for him and with those feelings came an incredible fear of loss.

Men didn't stick around once the pleasure had been spent. They didn't stay when the hard times hit. She'd learned that the hard way. With Kyle, she wanted to believe different. But how could she?

Twenty minutes later, she powdered herself, slipped into her clothes and decided to brave entering the kitchen.

"Is there any room in here for me?" she asked.

She was greeted with two wide grins inviting her to join them. It may be an illusion, she thought as she picked up the rolling pin, but the moment was too precious to ignore.

And Lauren wasn't quite ready to give it up. It had been so long since she had anything resembling family and Kyle had brought that into her life again. And introduced it to Kristen. Just for a little while, she wanted to savor the warmth he'd brought to their lives.

Many baked cookies and tied bows later, all the efforts of the day were finally completed. Lauren strung a strand of gold satin ribbon through the hole in the top of the last gingerbread cookie to be placed on the tree. After tying a big bow, she handed it to Kyle.

"You do the honors," she said.

"Why me?"

"You did so much work to make such a beautiful tree. You put on the last ornament."

"Too bad Kristen didn't stay awake long enough to do it herself." He placed the ornament on a branch just under the star.

"She must have played hard at your parents'. It isn't often

that she *asks* to go to bed. At least she got to put the aluminum foil star on the tree." She sighed. "Look at this tree."

"Yeah. Beautiful." She felt his eyes on her and a warm heat crept up her neck to her cheeks.

"After all the work you did while I was snoozing, it should be beautiful."

"I meant you."

She bowed her head, embarrassed by his compliment. But no, it wasn't embarrassment at all, was it? It was something much more. Her insides hummed and her head was light as a feather. Why did he always do this to her? She averted her gaze and stared at the Christmas tree.

"You look just like a little girl who's wishing on a star," he murmured.

"Do I? I don't feel very much like a little girl," she admitted, and yet in so many ways she knew she was still as naive and insecure as a child.

A deep chuckle bubbled up from his throat and he smiled, cocking his head to one side. The soft glow from the lights of the tree illuminated his face. His features were strong and sure. In his gaze, she saw the raw edges of desire. "But you're not a little girl, Lauren. You're a woman. An incredibly beautiful woman."

He brushed her cheek with the back of his hand. She involuntarily leaned into the source of pleasure.

She wanted him to hold her. It had been so long since she allowed herself to feel this vulnerable and exposed. Kyle was strong in body and in will and she needed his strength, needed *him*, more than she was ever willing to admit before.

"What do you dream of when you put your head down on your pillow at night? Tell me, Lauren," he whispered, pulling her into his arms, gazing down at her in a way she swore he could see straight through to her soul.

As she trembled in his arms, she knew if she opened her mouth to speak, it would be her undoing. The truth frightened her, the way he made her insides stir with the mere thought of him, the longing she had whenever he was gone.

No, she couldn't tell him the truth. If she did, then she'd have to tell him how she lay awake at night, longing to feel his hands run over every inch of her body. And how she wanted to return that pleasure. She'd tell him how she wanted to burn with the heat of his flesh and feel his heart racing wildly so close to hers.

That was her wish, her fantasy.

But she couldn't say a word, because she might just get her wish. And God help her after that.

"Kyle...I..." She closed her eyes and felt his lips brush against hers. At first, his kiss was like a gentle breeze blowing across her skin. Quickly it turned hot and hard, filled with a passion she'd never known. She burned with the intensity that melted her resolve. No amount of reasoning could convince her that she didn't want Kyle Preston.

And now he was here with her, holding her, kissing her with a wild abandon that made her forget all her fears.

~9~

Lauren felt Kyle's hard muscles flex beneath her touch as she leaned closer to his warm body. She looked up at him, into his eyes, and saw that his gaze was on her lips. She licked them instinctively and heard a guttural groan escape him. His desire was raw and transparent. It made her dizzy and catapulted her own desire skyward.

Was this really her? She wondered. She'd never thought of herself as a woman who could feel such deep emotional hunger. Or that she could bring forth such a response from a man.

Her past experience was nonexistent except for the one act that had produced her daughter. Although it had changed her life forever, it was over and done with before she even knew what was really happening. She was young then and didn't know the powerful effect that love could have on her.

Love.

Yes, this was definitely love, she realized. She was falling hopelessly in love with Kyle. This wasn't just about a physical need that had been left unfulfilled. It was about an emotional need she had no control over.

She hadn't known anything about love when she was eighteen. But what she knew now was that what she had with Kristen's father had never been love.

She didn't want that this time. She wanted to feel every touch, every breath, every nuance that made her know she was the woman that Kyle desired. And he did desire her. The thought of that rocked her world. Never in her life had she felt such power and yet felt so vulnerable at the same time.

He bent his head and kissed her lips softly, then withdrew. "You still have a cold."

She nodded. "I'm sorry."

He frowned slightly and shook his head. "No, no. Don't be. You concentrate on breathing. If you don't mind, I'll just take my time concentrating on you." And he did. She felt his hot breath scorch her neck as his lips brushed against her skin. She gasped and felt herself melt against him when he tugged at the soft flesh of her earlobe with his teeth.

She closed her eyes and flattened her hands, brushing her palms against his chest. Acting on impulse, she curled her fingers around the fabric of his shirt and pulled him toward the bedroom.

She looked up into his face and saw in his eyes what she felt in her heart. They shared a basic, primitive emotion that was so strong, nothing could divide it.

"My sweet Lauren." His voice was rough as he gazed into her eyes.

She reached up and framed his face in her hands. She'd never loved any man before. But she was in love with Kyle. What a frightening and wonderful revelation.

With the bedroom door safely closed behind them, he resumed his quest to concentrate on her. She tangled her fingers in his dark hair as he continued to kiss her neck, her cheek. When she felt his rough hand beneath the cotton fabric of her shirt, she sucked in a deep breath.

Kyle raised his head and looked at her, as if asking her permission to take this dance they'd started a step further. She gave him her answer as a smile. She arched her back as he reached behind her and undid the clasp of her bra.

With a low rumbling groan, he lifted her shirt off and lowered his head. The feel of his lips on her breast were like nothing she'd ever known. She wrapped her arms around his shoulders and pulled him down on the bed with her. They sunk into the mattress with the weight of Kyle's body laying along the length of hers. She lifted her hips to meet him. Beneath the fabric of his jeans, she felt his desire was strong and hard. He pressed himself against the cradle of her thighs in response and Lauren thought she'd die of torment.

In an instant, her longing to have him took over. She would have waited to follow his lead, after all, she couldn't say that she was completely sure of how to fulfill the desire she saw raging in him. Or felt in herself. But as she'd suspected all along, loving Kyle was as natural as breathing. Her love for him had taken control and washed away any fears lack of experience had given her.

She closed her eyes and felt his fingers tangle in her hair. As they kissed, she felt his tongue brush against her lips. He deepened their kiss and she welcomed the intimacy with each stroke, thinking about the promise of a deeper intimacy they were about to share.

She was nearly naked, except for her blue jeans and panties. And Kyle was completely dressed. She worked to change that fact.

She fumbled with his belt buckle until she was frustrated with her lack of success. "You do this," she panted. "Let me take care of your shirt."

With one swift motion, she pulled his shirt up to his shoulders, revealing a lattice of hard muscles. With him being so tall, she quickly realized the flaw in her plan and couldn't get the shirt any higher. But he deftly finished what she'd started, tossing the shirt to God knows where and dropping his jeans to the floor.

My Lord, but he was beautiful, she thought, gazing at him. Every inch of him was muscle and pure man. Her already raging body reached a fevered pitch and she moaned-she couldn't help it-when he stripped his briefs, revealing the strength of his desire.

Pulling the down comforter aside, she crawled on the bed and slipped off the last of her garments. "Come here," she said, holding her hand out to him.

He advanced toward her and abruptly stopped, turning toward his jeans instead of her. She watched impatiently as he sifted through his wallet, a worried look etched in his features, then a flash of relief before he pulled out a foil packet.

Her breathing grew more ragged as did his before he finally slid on top of her, their flesh burning with a passion almost to the brink of eruption. His hands stroked and caressed, his lips nipped and crushed, driving her skyward until she thought she'd go insane with need.

She wanted him inside her, to feel how close they could be. But she wasn't sure enough of herself to set the pace. Finally, she held his face in her hands and looked into his eyes. In them she saw a thousand promises meant to last a lifetime. She lifted her hips until they pressed against him in an erotic plea. And he instantly understood her unspoken words and smiled.

They came together like a tidal wave crashing against the shore. Her heart pounded with every breath, with each moan and cry, with each torturous stroke. They clung to each other until the first wave of release split her in two. She couldn't see or think or even breathe for what seemed like an eternity. Within seconds of floating back to reality, she felt every muscle in Kyle's body that was touching her grow hard until he, too, was taken over the edge of oblivion.

It took a few moments for her breathing to become even again and her mind to clear.

"Mommy?"

Panic struck Lauren hard in her chest when she heard Kristen's faint voice coming from the other room. She bolted upright in the bed.

"Mommy, I don't feel good."

Taking a few deeps breaths to compose herself, she watched for Kyle's reaction as she slid off the bed, grabbing the first thing she could find to cover her bareness.

He ran the fingers of both hands through his hair and looked at her. Was he upset? Did he understand that she would always give of herself as a mother first? As much as she wanted to stay in his arms, she couldn't let that get in the way of Kristen's needs.

"I'll be right there, honey," she called out. To her own ears, her voice was still shaky.

She took two steps toward Kristen's bedroom door and heard Kyle behind her, pulling on his clothes. She flicked the light switch as she walked into the room.

Kristen clutched her stomach and moaned. "I have a bellyache."

"How many cookies did you have today?" Lauren asked softly, then glanced at Kyle, who was now standing in the doorway, for confirmation.

He shrugged and wilted against the doorjamb. "We both ate quite a bit of dough while we were making the cookies this afternoon. Sorry."

Lauren frowned in disgust and sat on the edge of the bed. "No wonder you have a bellyache, sweetie," she said to Kristen as she rubbed her stomach.

"I'll get some ginger-ale," Kyle suggested.

When Kyle was out of earshot, Kristen tugged on Lauren's shirt, her eyes widened. "Are you going to marry Kyle?"

Completely taken aback, Lauren sat up straight and tried to steady herself. Where on earth had that come from? Had her little eyes seen something she shouldn't have? Oh, Lord, what had she done?

"Why do you ask?" Lauren probed.

"You look at him funny."

Her eyebrows furrowed. "Funny how?"

As if she were impatient, Kristen heaved an exaggerated sigh and said. "You know, the way Belle looks at the Beast in the video."

"I do?" she croaked.

Kristen nodded. "Julie says that sometimes people get divorced, just like a boy in my class, and they get new daddies."

"That happens sometimes."

"And Santa Claus said that all the other daddies are taken already."

"Well, honey-"

"And Julie said she never sees Kyle with a girl. Even though we didn't have a divorce, you could marry Kyle and he can be my new daddy. We can live together and be a family." She yawned before adding, "Wouldn't that be great?"

It would be wonderful, Lauren thought.

"Is that what you want, sweetie? You really want a daddy?"

Kristen nodded. "If you marry Kyle, will Julie be my sister?"

"The two of you were plotting more than a sleep-over, I see." Lauren's shoulders sagged and she puffed her cheeks. "I don't think we have to worry about all this just yet."

Kyle rapped on the door with his left hand and held a plastic cup in his right. "Everything okay?"

"Yeah."

She had no idea how long Kyle had been standing in the doorway or how much of their conversation he overheard. But by the look on his face and the slight tilt in his smile, she knew he heard enough.

He handed her the cup of ginger ale and settled onto the mattress at the foot of the bed. Kristen smiled her obvious pleasure.

If it hadn't been so delicate a situation, she may have allowed herself to feel lighthearted. What pained her was that no matter how hard she tried, she couldn't keep herself from doing just that. If anyone looked at them and didn't know any better, they'd think they were a family.

But that wasn't the case. They weren't a family. Who knew how long she and Kristen would be able to revel in all the delightful feelings Kyle Preston bestowed on them?

Still rubbing Kristen's belly, Lauren asked. "Any better?"

Kristen yawned and nodded, her eyelids at half mast.

"Goodnight, honey." She bent down and kissed Kristen's forehead. Kyle got up and did the same. He followed Lauren, turning the light off behind him before shutting the door.

She waited to speak before they were both alone in the living room. "You must be tired, too, after such a long day. I can't thank you enough, again, for all you've done."

"Are you trying to get rid of me already?" he teased, reaching for her.

She picked up his jacket and extended it to him. "You must be wanting to get home."

His smile faded when he saw she wasn't kidding. "You really do want me to leave?"

She took a deep breath, but said nothing.

He brushed his blond hair back with one swipe of his hand. "Is it what Kristen said about us getting married?"

"I'm sorry you heard that."

"I'm glad I did. At least I have one of you on my side." His gaze was searching as if he were trying to understand the about-face. And why wouldn't he be after what had just happened between them. If not for Kristen's call to Lauren, they'd still be in bed making love all night.

"This isn't about sides. I just think it's better this way," she said softly. "Kristen has never seen me with a man before. She's beginning to get the wrong idea."

His expression drooped. "Why do I get the feeling I did, too."

"She's not used to having family around. Suddenly, she's overwhelmed being with your family. Please don't get me wrong, I'm grateful for it. I've missed my own so much and, except for me, Kristen has never had that. But she's already asking me if she's going to be Julie's sister."

Kyle's face brightened. "We can accommodate her if she wants a sister."

"I'm serious."

"So am I."

Frustrated with the situation, she blew out an exaggerated breath. "You're missing the point."

"No, I don't think so. Kristen wants a family. And if you're honest with yourself, you want it, too."

She swallowed hard and averted her gaze.

"I could talk to your parents."

Her head snapped up and her eyes flew open wide. "And what, Kyle? Invite them to dinner? Is that your answer to everything?"

He lifted his arms in the air and let them fall clumsily to his side. "No, but it's a start, isn't it?"

"I won't let you do that. They've made their choice to stay out of my life despite my efforts. If that's the way it has to be, then so be it. It's not your problem."

"I'm making it my problem."

"For how long? I'm not some stray dog that wandered into your yard and scratched on your door."

He rolled his eyes. "Believe me. I don't put you in the same category as my dog."

"But I'm still a stray, aren't I? Are you going to make everything all right for me, then move on to the next person with a problem? When I'm no longer a problem?"

"What are you talking about?"

She touched one of the cookie ornaments on the tree before looking at him. She recalled how Kristen and Kyle had worked to decorate it with just the right amount of frosting and sprinkles. "Sooner or later, things aren't going to be as nice and pretty as they are today. It's inevitable. Then what? I don't want Kristen to get hurt."

"You're not talking about your daughter this time, Lauren. You're talking about yourself." He moved closer to her, but she backed up two steps. When she had the courage to look into his eyes, all she saw was pure pain. "Don't be afraid of us. I'm not like the other men in your life. I'm not going to leave you."

She laughed sardonically and mumbled under her breath, "That's exactly what they said."

"What do I have to do to prove to you that I'm not like them? Do I have to climb a mountain every time I walk through your front door? Because if that's what it takes, then I'm ready for the challenge."

"Don't you see? I don't want to be your challenge. When the challenge has been conquered, the game is over."

"Then tell me what you want."

"What I want doesn't exist. I want someone who's willing to stay for the long haul, when things are great *and* when they're ugly. I've never known a man that was willing to do that."

"You know me." He took her hand in both of his and kissed it lightly, then rested it against his cheek.

Easing her hand away, she said, "Really?"

She wasn't convinced. Kyle knew by the edge in her voice and heaviness in her eyes. What was it going to take to convince this woman how much she meant to him? To prove to her just how much he loved her?

"I was eighteen when I was adopted."

She looked at him, puzzled. "But I thought you were twelve."

"No. When I was twelve, my biological father went to court and relinquished me as his son so he wouldn't have to keep paying child support after my mother died."

He watched her horrified face. "Kyle, I'm so sorry."

"I don't remember much of my mother. I was younger than Kristen when she died. My father was married to someone else and didn't want me. I stayed with my grandmother until she couldn't care for me anymore. After that, I shifted from one distant cousin to an uncle or aunt for a few months until they couldn't handle me anymore and I went into foster care."

"It must have been awful for you."

"All you have to do is look at my childhood and you'll know how mistrust breeds."

"Judy and Will-" she started to say, but Kyle broke in.

"Are the best things that happened to me. And I almost blew that, too. After the accident, I was sure my *new* parents would throw me out of the house as soon as I turned eighteen. They had every right after the way I'd behaved. I figured I'd save myself the humiliation."

"What did you do?"

"I packed my bags and told them I was leaving." He shook his head. "I don't know what I was thinking. I suppose I thought they'd open the door and let me walk away and say 'Good Riddance'".

She shook her head and held her hands to her chest. "But they didn't, did they?"

He smiled and a flood of warmth filled his heart with the memory. "No, thank God. I remember my dad got angry and dragged me to the car, which was kind of hard since he's a full foot shorter than me. He didn't say a word until we got to his lawyer's office. Before we got out of the car, he told me I could go down to the bus station and leave. He'd even pay for the ticket. Or we could march into the lawyer's office and file the papers to make me his son legally."

Her mouth dropped open. "But why then? You were already legally of age."

"Exactly. There was no more red tape keeping them from adopting me. The state didn't care, but they did. My dad said he was there for the long haul, whether or not there was a piece of paper collecting dust in a courthouse somewhere saying he was or wasn't responsible for me. He said I'd always be his son." His voice cracked as he spoke. "That day it meant more than I can say to hear him call me son."

He saw a single tear trickle down Lauren's cheek, which she quickly brushed away with her fingers.

Kyle cleared his throat. "That's the kind of man he is and the kind of man I strive to be." He reached out to her again, hoping she'd welcome his touch, needing hers in return. She didn't back away this time. Instead, she wrapped her fingers around his hand and gave it a gentle squeeze. "I want to be here for you and Kristen. Some men mean what they say, Lauren. Some do stay."

"Your parents are wonderful people."

He nodded and couldn't help but smile. "I know your parents will come around. Whatever it is that is holding them back can be overcome."

She stiffened and pulled away, crossing her arms across her chest. "I'm glad you told me this, but-"

"But you don't believe me." He felt his heart fall through the floorboards.

She averted her gaze for a full five seconds before looking at him again. "I don't know what to think."

Somehow, someway, he had to get her to believe in him. It

was the only way she'd learn to trust his word. Damn every man who let her down before, but he wouldn't be one of them. And somehow, she would know that as fact.

He picked up his jacket and walked to the door. Bending down, he saw her close her eyes as he kissed her cheek. He breathed in her sultry scent, filling his head with tantalizing memories of how they lay so close to each other, making love just moments ago.

And he walked out the door. Not because that was what he wanted to do, but because that's what she wanted.

Once he was out on the bitter cold sidewalk, he turned and peered up at the top floor gable window of the Victorian home. Behind the curtain, he saw the soft glow from the light and a faint shadow of a silhouette standing by the window.

She was watching him leave her.

Because that was all she knew.

He climbed into the Jeep and jammed the key in the ignition until the engine roared. If this is what she wanted, then he would respect her wish and he'd leave.

For now. Only for now.

~10~

Lauren wiped her hands on the red cotton apron Judy had given her to wear. She looked around the kitchen and frowned when she saw there was no available counter space left. "Where do you want me to put this cake?"

Judy turned and search the same surface Lauren had just perused. "Mmm. There's no room in here until the food is cleared from the buffet table."

"I'll take it," Kyle said, walking through the kitchen doorway, munching on a pastry.

Judy swatted him on the arm with a dish towel. "I told you to wait until I serve."

Kyle returned a mischievous grin.

She picked up a two pastry dishes and headed for the kitchen door. "You'll go nowhere near that cake until dessert is served. Do you hear me?"

With Judy gone from the room, Lauren darted a glance at Kyle and held his gaze. His eyes were smiling as well as the rest of his face.

Relieved, she felt a smile tug at her own lips. After the way things ended the other night, she wondered how he would react to her. She thought about not coming. But a deal was a deal.

She promised him she would be here. And she *wanted* to be here with him.

When she'd stood at the window and watched him drive away two nights ago, she fought to keep herself from running down the stairs after him. She'd been tempted to tell him she wanted him to stay, that it didn't matter how long. She wanted to tell him how she felt.

But that was just it. What was she feeling? For the first time in years she allowed herself to think about herself as a woman with real emotions and desires. She'd been both exhilarated and frightened by the exigent need she had when Kyle held her, kissed her until he took her breath away. She would have allowed him to take her to the pinnacle of that need if she hadn't been pulled back to reality by Kristen's call.

And now, was it too late? Had she pushed him away too far?

As his smile danced in his eyes, she knew it wasn't. And she knew he was feeling the same thing, but it wasn't the right time to lose themselves. At some point, she would find the right moment and tell him, show him exactly how much she loved him.

"We haven't had so much as a moment to talk since I got here."

Kyle bent his head and kissed her cheek. "I know. We have a lot to talk about. There'll be some time tonight, after everyone's gone."

She bit her bottom lip to keep it from trembling. "We can pick up where we left off the other night," she whispered.

She watched his eyes grow dark and smoky, fueling her with the satisfaction that he knew what she meant.

"You're going to help me set up the doll house for Kristen, right?"

"You bet." He glanced at the kitchen clock and said, "I've got to go change. The kids are asking when Santa will arrive." He brushed by her and paused a moment to cup her cheek. His hand was rough against her skin and sent a tingling sensation through her body. She leaned into his touch before her eyes caught sight of Judy coming into the kitchen again.

Suddenly self-conscious, she straightened. But as if he understood her hesitation, Kyle didn't seem to mind. He bent down, kissing her lightly on the lips and said, "I'll be right back."

When he closed the kitchen door behind him, Lauren took a deep breath and glanced at Judy. Her approval was evident in the slight tilt of her mouth, and the twinkle in her brown eyes, but she said nothing.

"I guess I should go round up the troops," Lauren finally said.

Judy's smile widened and she gave a quick nod. "Good idea. And I'll dole out the dessert."

With the help of little Scotty, Will brought in an antique rocking chair with detailed scrolls carved into the back and placed it at the end of the room by the Christmas tree. It didn't take more than five minutes to gather all the kids in the house and settle them on the floor of the family room. Chas and his wife, Kim, whom Lauren had met briefly earlier in the evening, sat together on the loveseat with their youngest daughter. From the size of her, Lauren guessed her to be about two or three years old. Their eldest daughter was about the same age as Kristen and Julie.

When the room was set and Judy had finished setting all the pastries out on the buffet table in the dining room, they all sat...and sat...and waited.

Twenty minutes later, Santa Claus still had not arrived.

"Where is Kyle?" Judy whispered, so the children in the room wouldn't suspect.

"I know, he's been gone a long time." Lauren looked at the children sitting on the floor. They were fidgeting and beginning to get restless.

"I'll pass around the cookies. See if you can round up my so...ah, Santa," Judy said.

She nodded and weaved her way through the crowded room toward the kitchen. After pouring a glass of eggnog, she left the kitchen in search of Santa Claus. She did a walk through the downstairs of the house. There were small groupings of neighbors and friends talking in the formal living room, the dining room and the den, but Kyle was no where to be found.

As she rounded the corner toward the foyer, she met Kyle head on.

Or rather Santa Claus.

No wonder she hadn't recognize him in the parking lot the evening they met. The disguise was authentic, complete with lifelike white beard and hair. No one would recognize him beneath that red suit.

She held the glass of eggnog out to him. "You're late."

"You try stuffing yourself into this suit," he said, straightening his thick black belt. The disguise may have been convincing, but the voice was unmistakable, and lulling. She wondered what it would be like going to sleep each night having the deep sound of Kyle's voice be the last thing she heard before she fell asleep. And the first thing she heard in the morning when she woke up.

"You've got quite a crowd in there waiting for you."

He gripped the glass and took a long sip before handing the glass back. "I need my bag with the toys for the kids. Do you know where I left it?"

"In the kitchen. It's in the broom closet." She reached up and brushed his fake white beard with her fingers. "You dribbled."

"Thanks. Job hazard."

Zoey trudged through the foyer, dragging a pillow case filled with wrapped gifts. Lauren hadn't seen her all evening until now. Zoey tossed the bag to Kyle. "I'm not your little elf, Kyle," she grumbled.

"Hey, where's your holiday cheer?" he said as she climbed the stairs.

Zoey waved him off and kept going. Lauren hadn't recalled seeing Bruce hanging around either and wondered if his absence was the cause of her mood.

She turned to Kyle. "You ready?"

"As much as I'll ever be."

"You've got about twenty neighborhood kids sitting in the family room. If you don't get in there, there's going to be a kiddy revolt."

"Nah." He hoisted the bag of goodies on his shoulder and tested his ho ho's before weaving his way through the crowd of people now gathered in the family room. "Ho, ho, ho."

Although Lauren couldn't figure out how Judy managed it, all the kids were still seated on the floor and began to cheer when Kyle came into the room.

She watched as Kyle squeezed his stuffed body into the rocking chair. As he pulled the gifts from the pillowcase, he called out each child's name and they came up and sat on his lap.

After waiting so long, it took no more than fifteen minutes until everyone was done opening their gifts. "It's your turn, Mommy," Kristen said, tugging Lauren by the arm toward Kyle.

Kyle opened his arms wide. She could see a hint of mischief playing in his eyes beneath the white fluff he'd pasted to his eyebrows. Heat filled her cheeks as she looked around the room at the smiling faces of people she'd just met, urging her to sit on Santa's lap.

She hesitated a moment, feeling like she was a mannequin on display in a store window.

Kyle leaned forward in the rocker and pulled her to him, taking the decision out of her hands. She settled into his lap and felt her whole being melt.

"Did you cook this up with Kristen?" she asked, gazing in the depth of his blue eyes.

A rumble of laughter bubbled up from his throat.

"You're bad," she whispered in his ear, wrapping her arms around his neck, breathing in the scent of his aftershave.

He laughed seductively and darted his furry eyebrows up. "Do you want to find out how bad I can be?"

Oh, yes, she did. More than anything, she wanted to find out all she could about this man.

He cleared his throat and ho ho'd in a low rumble. But when he spoke to her, it was pure Kyle. "So, Lauren, tell me what you want for Christmas."

It may have been her imagination, but the noise in the room seemed to fade and she felt all eyes on her. But she never tore her gaze from Kyle. Beneath all the decoration and disguise, she saw the most incredible man she'd ever known. It was if all the fear of the past seven years, the shell of mistrust, melted like ice, leaving her able to see for the first time. And what she saw was the love of one hell of a man.

How could she think she could deny him?

Or herself?

She now knew he was the only thing she wanted. And she was totally and completely in love with Kyle Preston.

"Kyle...I-" she whispered, but she was cut off by Judy's voice calling her.

"I hate to interrupt, Lauren." She looked over at Judy, who was standing at the other end of the room holding the cordless phone in her hand. "You have a phone call."

Now who could that be? Lauren thought. No one but Mrs. Hopkins knew that she was planning to be here, and she hadn't given out the telephone number.

She looked at Kyle, his smile filled her with warmth.

"Go ahead," he urged gently.

"What is this?"

"It's going to be a great Christmas."

She cocked her head to one side and said, "Kyle, what'd you do?"

"Go ahead. I'll be waiting."

She eased off his lap and nervously brushed her hands down the skirt of her dress as she walked through the crowd, making her way toward the kitchen.

Judy handed her the phone. "The house is full of people, so there's not much in the way of privacy. But you might find a quiet corner upstairs," she made a sweeping gesture with her hand, "or here in the kitchen since everyone seems to have a full belly."

"Thank you." When Judy left the room, she turned away from the noisy family room and said, "Hello?"

For a few seconds, Lauren didn't hear any response. "Is anyone there?"

She was just about to hang up when she heard, "Hi, honey."

Emotion gripped her at the sound of her father's voice.

"Daddy? How did you..." She turned and saw Kyle standing in the family room talking to Chas. Of course, it had to be Kyle. How else would her parents have known to call her here?

"Honey, I'm..." She heard her father's voice crack. She tried to choke back her tears, but she just couldn't keep her emotions at bay. It was the first time in seven years hearing her father's voice. He cleared his throat. "I thought it was about time I called."

After all this time, she didn't know what to say. She filled her lungs with air before attempting to speak. "I'm...really glad you did. Did you get the picture of Kristen?"

His voice suddenly sounded lighthearted. "She's beautiful. She looks just like you."

"Yeah."

They were silent for a few agonizing moments. Like with her mother, Lauren feared the awkwardness that plagued them would win out.

"Ah...how on earth did Kyle track you down?"

"Kyle. Yes, he seems like a...persistent fellow."

She chuckled as a tear rolled down her cheek. "Well, he has that way about him."

"He said I should be proud of you, that you're a wonderful mother."

She swallowed hard. "I've really missed you, Daddy."

There was silence before he answered again. "Listen, honey, about what happened."

"No, Daddy. Let's not talk about that. It was a long time ago. Please, let's just start over." She didn't want to dredge up the past. It was better to leave all the bad feelings where they were and start anew.

"But you need to know that I never thought it would be like this. I never meant to make you feel we didn't care. It's just...somewhere along the way I'd forgotten how to reach out to you."

Hot tears streamed down her face. "I've always been here, Daddy."

She heard his muffled sobs. After a few seconds, her mother got on the line.

"Lauren?"

"Yeah, Mom, it's me." She held her hand to her mouth.

"Is everything okay, sweetheart?"

She sniffed and wiped her moist cheeks. "It could be. Mom, it's been so long. I have some time off of work next week and...I'd like to see you and Daddy...if it's okay."

"Next week?"

Lauren held her breath. "Yeah."

"I was hoping it could be sooner. That is if you don't mind. Kyle invited us to have Christmas dinner with you there."

Kyle was as tenacious as ever and she had to laugh at that. "Sounds like something he'd do."

Her mother cleared her throat. "Your father and I have talked about it. We won't come if you don't want us to."

"Oh, I want you to come. Please come. You won't believe how big Kristen is, and I know she'd love to meet you." She gulped back a sob. "We have a lot of catching up to do, don't you think?"

"Yes, I think it's time. I love you, honey."

Lauren closed her eyes. Simple words that meant so much. "Me, too. I'll see you tomorrow."

She hung up the phone and took a deep breath. It was a start. One small step that alone they were never able to make. But Kyle had made it possible.

Looking through the doorway, she saw Kyle was still in the other room talking to Chas. Knowing her makeup was probably all over her face by now, she decided to go upstairs to the guest room and freshen up before talking with him.

"It's good seeing you, buddy," Chas said, slapping Kyle on his back.

"Me, too. I'm sorry things didn't work out in New Jersey."

He shrugged uncomfortably.

Chas waved him off. "At least I don't have to listen to Kim complain about how much she never sees the family anymore."

As Chas talked about his plans, Kyle glanced through the doorway at Lauren. She stood with her back to him. One hand was on the phone, the other was touching her face. Right then, he would've done anything to know how she'd reacted to her father's telephone call.

If it hadn't been for Mrs. Hopkins being able to remember that Lauren had come from Syracuse, he never would have been able to track them down. He remembered she mentioned her parents were psychologists. He called every number in the Syracuse phone book until he tracked them down. It took him half the day, but three quarters of the way through the listings, he found them.

At first, Samuel Alexander was less than enthusiastic about talking to a total stranger about his daughter and refused to speak to him on the phone. But Kyle wouldn't be put aside. It was much too important to Lauren. If he could help them mend their fences, then it was worth doing anything it took to make it happen. He got in the Jeep and drove all the way to Syracuse to meet with them. Only then did Lauren's parents see how serious he was and finally agreed to talk to him.

Turning back to Chas, he asked, "Do you have anything lined up yet?"

Chas shook his head. "With the baby due in a few weeks, I figured I'd just wait until after Kim delivers and help her for a week or so with the girls. I've got my sights set on that property over in Belchertown. You know, the one that was abandoned a few years ago."

"Yeah, it's been on the market a while."

"Well, I have some ideas for a re-hab project you might be interested in getting in on. I could use your help putting it together."

Kyle smiled. It felt like old times. Except now, their partnership had nothing to do with trouble. "When you're ready to talk business, let me know."

Chas glanced over at his family and smiled with affection. "Fate has a funny way about her, doesn't she?"

"Are you getting philosophical in your old age?" Kyle teased.

"Hey, who are you calling old?" Chas gave a mock punch to Kyle's stuffed suit. "Beer belly and white hair. Look at you. You look like hell."

He laughed along with Chas, but stopped short when the laughter faded. "Do you ever wonder what things would be like for us if we'd never been in that accident?" he asked, suddenly uncomfortably. After all this time, Kyle truly believed they'd gotten past what had happened that awful night. But unlike Chas, Kyle's life had been turned around for the better. Chas had all his hopes and dreams stripped from him. "You regret losing that scholarship?"

Chas chuckled, shaking his head. "Hell, no. If I'd gone off like I'd planned, I'd probably be working too many hours, divorced, giving all my money to an ex-wife who'd love spending it."

"No, seriously."

"I am. If I could go back and change things, I wouldn't do it. It was fate. If that accident never happened, I never would have met Kim and we wouldn't have what we have." Chas glanced over at Kim, who was sitting on the sofa with a coffee cup on her belly. The kids were gathered all around her, staring intently at her belly until the little bundle inside kicked the cup off. "Kim and the girls are the best thing that ever happened to me. I wouldn't trade them for anything in the world. All in all, I'd say I'm truly blessed."

Kyle smiled, feeling his heart lift a notch. "I'm really happy for you."

Chas motioned toward the kitchen. "She seems like she fits right in here. You might want to think about settling down yourself."

Kyle looked over and saw Lauren was now off the phone. "I'm working on it."

She turned in their direction, and he saw her wiping her cheeks. She was crying. Crying. His heart plummeted as she turned and ran from the kitchen. What had he done?

Chas shook Kyle's hand. "I've got to get my little princesses home." He lowered his voice. "This Santa has some bicycles to put together before morning. We'll see you soon?"

"You bet."

Kyle couldn't wait any longer. He had to find out how things went with Lauren and her parents. Seeing how upset she was, it didn't look good. After giving a quick search to the rooms downstairs, he groaned inwardly. She was gone.

Most all the other guests had either left or were saying good-bye at the door. As he rounded the corner of the family room, he saw Julie and Kristen sitting cross-legged on the floor, playing with the paper dolls they'd gotten as a gift. But he still couldn't find Lauren.

Why hadn't he listened to her and stayed out of this business with her parents like she asked? After he'd hung up the phone with them this afternoon and learned that they'd agreed to make amends, he was sure he'd made the right decision in going to see them. They were finally willing to try to work out their problems. It seemed like everything was going his way. Now he wasn't so sure. Maybe he'd just made matters worse.

~11~

Lauren pulled the flowered comforter up to Kristen's chin and kissed her cheek. "Did you have a good time tonight?"

Kristen nodded, already half asleep.

She kissed her goodnight and flicked off the light on the night stand before lightly walking across the room. She started to close the bedroom door when she saw Kristen's bolt upright in bed. From the light streaming in from the hall, she saw how wide and luminous her little girl's eyes were, searching for the answers to something as if it lay heavy on her mind. She swung the door open again. "What is it, hon?"

"Do you think Santa Claus will really be able to find us here?" Kristen asked.

Lauren immediately felt a lump in her throat, but tried to appear nonchalant when she answered. "Yes, of course. He already saw you here tonight, didn't he?"

"Mommy, that was Kyle," Kristen replied, whispering as if she didn't want anyone else to hear.

"Oh, well..." She padded across the floor and eased herself down on the mattress next to Kristen. "Then I guess I'm just going to have to call Santa and tell him where we are."

The skeptical look on Kristen's face told Lauren that she

wasn't sure of that answer, either.

Lauren decided to try another approach. "There is going to be a special surprise for you tomorrow."

Kristen perked up. "You mean Santa is really going to bring me a daddy?"

Her smile was so bright, it made Lauren's heart ache. She'd been ready to tell Kristen that she would meet her grandparents for the first time. Lauren had always talked of her parents and kept their picture displayed. Kristen would periodically asks questions about her grandparents, but tomorrow they would become real to her. It was what Lauren had dreamed of for so long.

But that was not what Kristen truly wanted.

This thing with Kyle was so brand new. There was no telling where it would lead them. Lauren wanted to give it all she had to give. But having a relationship with Kyle didn't mean Kristen would get her Christmas wish for a daddy. She only hoped that come Christmas morning, Kristen wouldn't be too disappointed.

"Honey, I don't think that's possible."

Kristen's eyelids drooped and her lips pouted. "I know," she said softly. "Santa Claus already told me all the daddy's were taken."

Lauren heaved a sigh and tried to sound cheerful. "I know there will be something special from Santa tomorrow morning. But you can't get your present if you don't go to sleep."

Instead of questioning her mother again, Kristen gave an idle nod and lay her head back down on the feather pillow. Lauren kissed her on the forehead and left the room.

A few minutes later, she pranced into the living room to join Will and Judy, who were already setting up their Santa display.

"I hope you don't mind, we already started," Judy said. "No matter what time they go to bed, Julie and Scotty will be up at the crack of dawn."

Will chuckled, fatigue pulling at his features. "And so will the rest of the house." He pointed to the cardboard box sitting next to the sofa. "Kyle carried your box in for you."

Lauren felt giddy with delight. The living room, like the rest of the home, was beautifully decorated. Stockings hung along the stone fireplace, each one embroidered with the names of all the family members. She smiled when she saw that Judy had added stockings for her and Kristen. Earlier, Kristen had been quick to point out that she recognized her name next to Julie's. The tree was still lit with tiny white lights and literally covered with glass ornaments. The formal appearance of this tree was a sharp contrast to the one they'd decorated at her apartment just days before. But it held its own unique charm. Beneath the tree, Judy and Will placed packages wrapped in every imaginable color and design.

A rendition of *I'll Be Home for Christmas* by Johnnie Mathis played softly on the stereo. Lauren filled Kristen's stocking with the few odds and ends she'd purchased and swallowed a large lump in her throat. For the first time in years, Lauren felt as if she were part of a family. And tomorrow would bring her closer to her own.

She started to tie the big red satin bow she'd purchase at the linen store around the doll house and stopped. Looking around the room and down the hall, she realized something, or rather someone, was missing. It just didn't seem right setting up the doll house without Kyle. After all, he was the one who made this gift possible. Where was he?

She finished tying the bow and lifted herself from her awkward kneeling position on the floor.

"I'm going to get some water. Can I get anything for anyone?" Lauren asked.

"No, thank you," Judy said, the fatigue of the day finally beginning to show on her face.

Will shook his head and kept on studying the directions for constructing one of the kid's toys.

It was nearly two thirty, she noticed, when she made her way past the grandfather clock in the foyer and to the kitchen. Her aching toes started to protest loudly after being in heels for so long and her pantyhose were uncomfortable. She couldn't wait to change out of her clothes and get into a pair of old sweats, but all that would have to wait. She needed to see Kyle first.

If she could only *find* him.

Zoey was in the kitchen when she poked her head through the doorway. She was barefoot and her oversized team T-shirt hung just above her knees.

"Did the Santas finish up or am I still banned from the living room," Zoey said, taking a glass from the cabinet. She opened the refrigerator and poured herself a glass of orange juice. In the dim light from the lamp above the sink, Lauren noticed her eyes were puffy and red.

"I'm surprised you're still up," she said.

"There's only so much sleeping a person can do before it gets old. Do you want some?" Zoey held out the carton of orange juice and waited for a reply before placing it back in the refrigerator.

Lauren shook her head. "Bruce didn't show up tonight?"

Zoey slumped back against the counter. "I think Kyle scared him off." She sighed and looked as if she were on the verge of tears. "Who am I kidding, he probably had something better to do than hang out here. You can't count on a man for anything, can you?"

Up until a few hours ago, Lauren probably would have agreed with Zoey.

But not anymore.

"I'm sorry things didn't work out. But that doesn't mean it never will." Her words sounded lame, even to her own ears. She'd heard those same words before, over and over, but never believed them. "You know, you remind me of myself a little when I was your age."

Zoey chuckled and pulled at her spiked hair. "Yeah, minus the Technicolor hair and pierced everything."

Lauren couldn't help but laugh. "Yeah, you're right. But I would have given anything to have a big brother to look after me the way Kyle looks out for you."

Zoey deposited the glass in the sink and swung around to

face her. "Be my guest. You can have him."

Nothing would make me happier.

"Speaking of Kyle, do you know where he is?"

Zoey motioned out the window. "He went back to the carriage house a little while ago to change. Said he was going to turn in. The lights are on. He's probably still awake if you want to head over."

Her shoulders sagged. Why hadn't he waited for her as they'd planned? "I don't want Kristen to wake up and find I'm not here," she said quietly.

"She did fine the other night when she was here. She probably won't wake up until Scotty drags us all out of bed at five in the morning." She rolled her eyes, then smiled, softening her expression. "She'll be okay. I'll check in on her. It's not like I'm doing much of anything else."

Lauren hesitated a minute. "Okay, thanks Zoey."

She grabbed her coat from the closet in the foyer and slipped out the kitchen door. The moonlight was bright and her body cast a shadow on the pebble stone path as she walked. But the path remained well lit. Her high heel shoes dug into the gravel and crunched with each step. Or maybe that was her toes. They were bunched up from being in her heels all evening and were now cold. But even with the frigid temperature outside, it was amazing how warm she felt inside now that she finally knew love.

There had been plenty of times when she never thought she'd find love in her life. Many times when she felt there was no room in her heart to love anyone but Kristen. But she had been wrong. Thank God she'd been wrong and found a man like Kyle Preston to show her how good love could really be.

That is, if he'd still have her after all the pushing away she'd done.

As she pulled the outer carriage house door closed and started up the long staircase to Kyle's apartment, anticipation raced through her veins. Each step was taking her closer to fulfillment, closer to the love she never thought she'd have.

She knocked lightly on the wooden door and strained to hear an answer. *Please let him be awake,* she prayed silently.

"It's open," she heard him call from inside, and her heart skipped a beat. She eased the door open, hearing the hinges creak slightly, and stepped inside.

It was dim in the apartment, she noticed as she made her way passed the bedroom and down the hall toward the living area.

When she saw him, she said, "You disappeared on me. I thought you were going to help with the doll house?" Even to her own ears, her voice sounded uncertain.

Kyle was seated in a recliner facing the wood stove. Max was sprawled out on the floor by his side. When she walked into the room, he looked at her, then turned his gaze to the dog and stroked his thick fur. "I went looking for you...after you got the phone call, but you weren't anywhere around. After a while I figured maybe you didn't want to be found, so I came back here."

"I had to get Kristen ready for bed." She stood by the counter in the kitchen, and he was way too far on the other side of the room for her comfort. "You know, she knew it was you playing Santa tonight."

From the wood stove's fire glow, she saw his half grin, but he didn't answer or look her way. He just held his gaze down and stroked Max fur. She still couldn't be sure he was happy that she'd come here at all.

In an instant, Lauren forgot her reasoning, replaced by sheer impulse that was foreign to her. She didn't recognized the womanly impulse she was acting on or the woman she'd become. But it felt good and natural and being with Kyle had made that metamorphosis.

She exhaled slowly. "It's been a long time since I've felt part of a family." She dropped her coat on the back of the kitchen chair and willed herself across the room. Kyle made no move to meet her. She wondered just what he was thinking, maybe why she'd come to see him this late at night, what her intentions were.

He lifted his head with her motion. Their eyes met and held

for a lingering moment and Lauren thought it would last a lifetime. He still didn't speak. He just gazed at her, a thousand different emotions flashing across the strong features of his face.

"I was...thinking...you know, that you..." Lauren stammered, then puffed her cheeks. "Oh, boy."

"I know. Me, too." His baritone voice swept across the room, singing softly in a way that filled her soul. "I've been doing a lot of thinking tonight."

She flipped a lock of hair behind her ear and with her fingers, followed the strand down until she reached its end, just above her breast. "You called my parents-"

"Don't," he said tersely, looking down at Max lolled on the floor. "I know I had no right to go against your wishes, no matter how good my intentions were. I wanted you to have a special Christmas. I wanted you to be with your family again. I thought I could help. And now I've-"

"I'm so glad you did," she cut in.

His head shot up and his expression was one of pure shock.

"I'm glad you didn't listen to me. In seven years we haven't managed to get as far as we did tonight."

"But I saw you. You were crying. I thought I'd-"

She smiled, feeling her bottom lip quiver. "They were happy tears, Kyle."

His chest heaved with a sigh and the muscles of his face smoothed instantly, as if he were relieved. In the light from the fire, she saw the glistening of tears in his eyes. "I thought I'd messed up everything for you."

"Tomorrow, Kristen will finally meet her grandparents and have a real family Christmas. I'm a little nervous about how things are going to go. Scared to death, in fact. It's been so long since I've seen my parents, but you've helped give us a start and for that I'm so grateful." She shrugged. "Who knows? We may just be okay, after all."

Kyle smiled, then bolted from the chair and met her half way across the room, pulling her into his arms in a tight embrace. He felt so good, so alive, so comforting. She breathed in his scent, intensely masculine and inviting, absolutely arousing all her senses. She couldn't imagine how she'd made it this far without his strength and now she knew she couldn't live without it.

Her cheek was pressed against his shoulder, her eyes closed. "I'm sorry about what happened the other night at my apartment. I...was scared."

He kissed her head. "I know. But you don't have to be. Not with me."

"I know that now. I missed you that night when you left. And every night since."

"Then stay with me now. Let me hold you like I should have held you then."

That was all she needed to hear him say. Taking a step back, she unzipped the back of her dress and waited. Kyle tucked his fingers beneath the delicate fabric and pulled it down to reveal the bare skin of her shoulders. Gravity took hold of the dress and pulled it to the floor, where it puddled at her feet.

The hunger in his eyes was fierce and matched the pounding of her heart. His breathing turned quick and rough when she took his hand and pulled him toward the bedroom. They reached the door and she heard prancing paws on the kitchen floor. Kyle swung around for a second and warned, "Not on your life, Max." Then closed the door behind them.

~12~

Lauren rolled over on her side and ran her index finger across Kyle's brow as he slept. She was in love with Kyle Preston. It was an incredible feeling.

Snuggling closer, she bent down and kissed his cheek. His response was immediate as he wrapped his arm around her, pulling her close to his naked body, tangling his legs with hers.

"Merry Christmas, Lauren," he murmured in that deep tone she found so sexy, his eyes still closed.

She smiled. Yes, it was a very Merry Christmas, indeed. For all of them. She kissed him again, this time full on the lips and breathed in his scent, mingled with the scent of sex from the warm sheets.

"I hate to do this, but I need to get out of here," she murmured.

His eyes flew open and he lifted out of bed, resting the full weight of his upper body on his arms.

Lauren chuckled. "Don't worry. I just need to get back into the guest room before anyone wakes up. I have a six year old daughter, remember?"

He smiled and sank back onto the pillow. "I guess it wouldn't look very good for you to be strolling in the house wearing last night's party dress when everyone is in their pajamas." He reached over and pulled her to him. "Personally, I'd rather be out of my pajamas with you."

Her head felt as light as a feather and she giggled. "I like the sound of that, too. But we have to hurry. We have a big day ahead of us."

"Are you nervous about seeing your parents?"

She hesitated. "A little."

"It's going to be okay."

Lauren knew Kyle was right. He had to be right. "First we have to get through Christmas morning. I want to be there when the kids wake up. I can't wait to see Kristen's face when she sees the doll house."

"Me, too."

The room was just starting to get light as the sun rose over the hills. As she threw the blankets off her body, the cold air chilled her skin, warm from snuggling so close to Kyle, and caused goosebumps to raise on her bare skin.

"Where are my clothes?" she muttered, searching on the floor for her pantyhose and underwear, discarded last night in their haste to make love.

"I think your dress is still in the other room. At least, I hope it's still there. Max was loose all night."

"Oh, no! How am I going to sneak back in to the house unnoticed without my dress? What if someone is awake and they see me?"

Kyle started to laugh.

"What are you doing?" she scowled teasingly, trying to wiggle into her pantyhose and bra. "What am I going to wear?"

"I'll give you a sweatshirt," she heard Kyle say as she ran into the living room to search for her dress. Despite her initial horror, she found her dress on the floor by the leather sofa, apparently spared by the dog's teeth.

The shades to the bay window were open and Lauren caught the first poking of the sun up over the horizon. After wiggling into her dress, she turned to find Kyle standing behind her wearing a pair of blue sweatpants.

"What I wouldn't do to crawl back into bed with you," she said, brushing her hand down his washboard stomach.

"I know. But if I know Scotty, he's probably already knocking on my parent's bedroom door, begging them to see if Santa came."

"You'll be right behind me?"

"All the way."

Lauren could hardly contain her excitement as she ran back to the house. Christmas morning was here. So many possibilities lay ahead.

It always amazed Kyle how much time it took to wrap all the gifts for Christmas and how little time it took for everyone to tear them apart. He'd caught Lauren worrying her bottom lip when Kristen sat down in front of the doll house. But any fear of Kristen's disappointment was dispelled when Kristen's whole faced beamed. Yanking on her mother's arm, Kristen pulled Lauren to the floor, and they proceeded to spend the morning rearranging all the miniature furniture inside each tiny room. He didn't think he'd ever forget Lauren's radiant smile and how happy she was at that moment.

Kristen's strong desire for a daddy had been put aside. At least, for the time being. There was plenty of time later in the day to put his plan in motion. Then they'd all have their Christmas wish.

Judy had pushed dinner to later in the day to allow Lauren's parents time to drive down from Syracuse. Lauren chewed on her fingernails and peeked out the window more times than Kyle could count. He knew the instant Samuel and Brenda Alexander arrived.

"They're here," she said breathlessly, turning to him with tears in her eyes. "How do I look?"

He walked with her to the foyer and kissed her before opening the door. "Beautiful. You go on. I'll get Kristen."

Lauren clutched her stomach as she opened the front door. She was glad Kyle had taken care of getting Kristen. It would give her a few minutes alone with her mom and dad before they met the rest of the Preston clan.

As always, her mother waited inside the car until her father came around to open the passenger door. Tears spilled from her eyes with the sight of them. Her father was older than she remembered. His hair was more silver than black now. He'd taken off his overcoat during the long ride. Lauren guessed he wore a size or two larger that he had seven years ago. As her mother stepped out of the car, she saw how the years had taken its toll, but Brenda Alexander was still as beautiful as Lauren remembered.

All fear of her parent's rejection was cast aside when Brenda opened her arms to Lauren. Lauren ran to her. The arms she never thought would hold her, clutched her tight. Samuel placed his arms around the two of them and they huddled in the driveway for a long overdue embrace.

"I'm so glad you're here," Lauren said, sniffing back happy tears.

"Me, too," Brenda cried.

"Where is my beautiful granddaughter?" Samuel asked.

Lauren couldn't help but giggle. She'd waited so long for this moment. "She's inside with Kyle. Come on and meet the Prestons. You'll like them."

She walked up the driveway arm in arm with Brenda. Samuel walked on her other side of Lauren, a bundle of brightly wrapped presents in his arms.

Brenda tugged at her. "Kyle seems like a good man."

She looked up and saw Kyle standing on the porch, holding Kristen in his arms. Words didn't describe how she felt about Kyle Preston. She swallowed the lump in her throat. "Yes, Mom, he is a very good man."

"I'm happy you found him."

Lauren could have told her that Kyle had been the one to find her broken down in an empty parking lot. He'd rescued her that night. In more ways than one. Did he really know what he'd done? She'd have to make a point to tell him in her own special way.

They all walked into the house together and introductions were made. Judy and Wally stayed back as Lauren introduced Kristen to her grandparents.

"This is Grandma and Grandpa, Krissy."

Kristen clung to Lauren and stared at her grandparents. Lauren had expected as much and hoped her parents were hurt by Kristen's shy reaction.

Samuel took Kristen by the hand and said, "Do you see this bag? I'll bet you can find a present or two in here with your name on it. You want to sit down with your Grandma and Grandpa and take a look?"

Kristen peered up at Lauren with a weary expression.

"It's okay, honey. I'm right here."

Lauren stayed by Kristen's side as she unwrap more gifts. She was aware of Kyle's gaze the whole time. When it looked as though Kristen was comfortable being doted on by Brenda and Samuel, Lauren went to Kyle's side.

"Thank you for this," she said, taking his hand, knowing she could never adequately express her feelings for all he'd given her.

He wrapped his arms around her waist and kissed her head. "You got your Christmas wish."

"And what about you, Kyle? What's your Christmas wish?"

He breathed deeply and she felt his chest press firmly against her breast. He tipped her chin with his fingers so she'd meet his gaze. "I have everything I want right here in my arms."

She sighed. "It's not just me. This is a package deal."

"I wouldn't have it any other way. I love that little girl as much as if she was my own flesh and blood."

"I know. I just needed to hear you say it."

Kyle bent his head and kissed her. "I have something for you," he murmured against her lips.

She chuckled softly. "Kyle, you've done enough. What

more could I possibly need or want?"

"For us to be a family. I can't think of anything I'd want more."

She gazed into his eyes and saw the promise of forever. "You're serious."

He pulled a velvet box from his pocket. The room went still as if everyone was focused on the two of them alone. Kyle opened the box to reveal a sparkling diamond solitaire.

"Oh, Kyle," Lauren gasped.

He placed the ring on her trembling finger, and she peered at it through tear-filled eyes.

"This was my Christmas wish. I love you and I want us to be a family." He took a deep breath and held her, pressing her hard against his body.

"I love you, too. So much."

"Now maybe we could find a way to make Kristen's Christmas wish come true."

"You mean it, Kyle?" Kristen squealed from the other side of the room. Everyone in the room started to laugh.

Kyle crouched down to Kristen's level, and she ran to him, wrapping her arms around his neck.

"Would you like me to be your daddy?"

Kristen beamed up at Lauren, as if hoping to get approval. When Lauren smiled and nodded, Kristen jumped up and down and said, "You bet!"

The next moments were filled with hugs and kisses from the whole family congratulating them on their engagement. Julie and Kristen were giggling about being sisters. Judy and Brenda laughed about how wonderful it was to have a wedding to look forward to in the coming year. And Samuel and Wally were busy getting acquainted.

Lauren couldn't remember ever feeling as happy as she did at that moment.

Kyle drew up behind her, resting his hand on her shoulder. "You got quiet all of the sudden. Are you feeling a little overwhelmed?"

"Never. Just appreciating my blessings."

"We've got a lifetime of those ahead."

"I'm so glad. Merry Christmas, Kyle."

He wrapped his arms around her and pulled her against him, kissing her long and forcefully. She had a family again and a lifetime of kisses from a man that took her breath away. Who could ask for anything more?

About the Author . . .

Although she's been writing novel length fiction for three years, Lisa Mondello has been writing for as long as she can remember. In the early days it was short stories and poetry for herself until her love for reading and writing was fed by her sister, Maria, when she took home a Harlequin Romance. Lisa's been an avid reader of romance novels of all sub-genres ever since and dreamed of one day writing a romance novel herself.

She attended the University of Lowell in Massachusetts for Sound Recording Technology before moving on to manage a local Boston rock band for four years. The band achieved regional success, winning a number of band competitions, recording several EP's and landing a spot on the infamous M-TV with Julie Brown.

She has been married for eight years to the man responsible for giving her a gentle nudge back into writing. Her husband Tom informed her she might enjoy writing a romance novel as much as she enjoyed reading them. Was he ever right!

Lisa now writes full time, switching between romance novels, articles on writing and her electronic book column with The Lover's Knot Magazine. In 1999 she will add her workshop on Electronic Books to the list, educating readers and writers on this new medium by speaking at conferences and booksignings.

All I Want for Christmas is You is Lisa's first published romance novel and holds a special place in her heart because it is set in the Western Massachusetts town she now resides in with her family.

A little bit about Neighborhood Press

The dream of giving new authors a place to showcase their work in an shrinking market drove Rhea Griffiths to create Neighborhood Press in 1993. Armed with her desktop computer, and little more than the will to succeed, she has come from producing one title her first year to a full twelve titles five years later.

As a leader in the electronic publishing industry, Neighborhood Press continues to excel, and offer the reader as well as the writer a new place to find exciting, well written fiction they will enjoy even after they have closed the books.

In an effort to do everything possible to treat their authors with the hard work and dedication they deserve, Neighborhood Press prints and binds their own books, and is constantly seeking ways to set their books apart from others, including the use of inventive paper stock and art work, like you find in this book.

If you have any comments or suggestions, please contact the publisher at:

Neighborhood Press
5341 Otter Lane
Middleburg, Fl 32068

And be sure to check out our web page at:
http://members.aol.com/nppubs for a listing of our other great titles!

Santa Claus is going to have a rough season...

Lauren Alexander is raising her daughter alone. Abandoned by her family for her decision to keep her daughter Kristen, she has done a pretty good job for the last six years. Or she thought she had. That's why she is crushed when little Kristen gives up her wish for a toy or goodie, and instead asks Santa for a present for her mother. But delivering Daddies isn't usually Santa's Bag.

This Santa has a plan...

Kyle Preston knows what it's like to be abandoned too. Luckily he found the support of loving adoptive parents and has turned himself into one of the most affluent real estate developers in town.
Building a house is easy. Building someone's trust is a whole different story. But a little Christmas magic can make all the difference in the world...

ISBN 1-891308-01-5
Retail Price $10.00 (US)
Special Price $8.00
Collectible Limited Copy

Lisa Mondello